Praise for Illusion
Book One of The Illusion Trilogy

"For such a young writer, it was very good... **I could see glimmers of true talent in this book.**"

-*New York Times* Bestselling Author, Tawni O'Dell

"I'm so impressed with Ms. Rodgers' *Illusion*. A **page turner** that is geared toward young adults, **it is a great read for anyone.** Definitely one to add to your to-read bookshelves!"

-Dana Faletti, bestselling author of *The Whisper Trilogy* and *Beautiful Secret*

"The most creative book I've read in a long time."

"*Illusion* is suspenseful, gripping, and surprising from beginning to end, making it **the definition of a 'page-turner.'**"

-Holly at *Nut Free Nerd*

"*Illusion* is an extremely well-written and interesting read. Nadette **created characters who are both relatable and feel very real.** The story is also captivating and keeps you guessing what is real and what is just a dream the entire time you're reading."

-J.T. Philips, author of *The Legacy Series*

"Wow, what an impressive new young writer who already has stirred things up in people's minds and hearts in her first book *Illusion*! Readers will get lost in her intriguing and inspired writing style.** This is one fantastic read, and I could not put it down. This is saying a lot from someone who does not normally read these styles of books and this genre. You see I am a business man and a number one best selling author of my own business book. I normally tend to read fact based business books. **But this author and these series of books has just changed all that."**

-#1 Amazon Bestselling Author, Stephen D. Rodgers

"Rodgers perfectly captures the teenage experience and voice."

"Well-paced, humorous, and delightfully surprising, Illusion promises to capture the reader's attention from page one to the very end ... **brings a whole new dimension to the world of YA fiction!"**

-Emily at *The Obstinate Owl*

"Captivating!"   "I couldn't put it down!"   "Compelling."

"You know when a book is so intriguing and **you can't stop reading**? That's what happened with this book."

-Nino at *Enchanted Readers*

"Jaw-dropping ending!"   **"An unexpected surprise."**

Echo

Book Two

Nadette Rae Rodgers

Printed in the United States of America

ISBN: 0692909788
ISBN: 978-0692909782
Library of Congress Control Number: 2017909933
Nadette Rae Rodgers, Cranberry Township, PA
CreateSpace Independent Publishing Platform
North Charleston, South Carolina

To my Nana, Rita Rodgers, who I can only see in my dreams. You'll be forever in our memories.

"A broken heart isn't so much the loss of the person as it is the loss of your dreams with that person."

-unknown

Prologue
- Addison -
Friday, May 25th, 2018

"Jessica Elizabeth Clark," the principal announced. Jess got up from her folding chair, golden hair falling just above her shoulders. I still couldn't believe she cut it so short; I was always so jealous of her perfect hair.

She glanced back and locked eyes with me. She winked, and I smiled back. Jess and I have come a long way. We are actually pretty good friends now. Cammie still hates her guts though. But Jess and I have a connection through our dreams that I'll never have with Cam. Cammie is still my best friend, but it's nice to have someone to talk to who gets it.

She walked with such gracefulness across the stage. She looked regal, like a princess about to be coronated. Her red gown floated as she walked. Her cap fixed perfectly. She probably wouldn't even have hat hair when she took it off. Somehow, she managed to find heels the exact red as the cap and gown. *Only Jess,* I thought.

If you would have told me a year ago that I would be leaving soon on a trip with Jess for the summer, I would have told you you were crazy.

But I am.

Jess and I are going backpacking through Europe. We leave next Friday.

Of course, my mother wouldn't okay the trip unless she came. *She's seen too many thriller movies, in my opinion.* So, Mom is coming with me and Jess to Europe. I really wish my aunt Carrie would come with us, but after everything that has happened in the last year and a half I think it's just too much for her.

So, the journals did have some interesting information in them after all. That's how I got the idea for the trip. That's also how I found out so much about my aunt, because God knows she wouldn't tell me anything herself.

I also would have called you crazy a year ago if you would have told me what my senior year of high school held.

I liked to think I had my life together.

Actually, no, I didn't.

My dreams are proof of that. They are anything but normal. But that's why I'm going on this journey. I'm hoping one of the places we visit will hold some answers, or better yet, healing.

"Cameron Margaret Fuller," my best friend's name pulled my mind back to the present.

I clapped and cheered and tears threatened to escape my eyes as I watched my best friend in the whole world walk across the stage. I actually couldn't believe we did it. We graduated high school!

She looked up and I waved. I looked to the side and saw her mom giving her a big thumbs up, so proud of her little girl.

Cammie would be attending our state's university, a few hours away from Madison, and she planned to study nursing. I think she'd make a really great nurse, actually. She's really compassionate and caring.

Then I sat there for the next half hour, listening to the list of names, some kids I had talked to, others I really hadn't. I thought about my life so far, especially the past year and a half, and I thought about the future, wondering what it would hold for me. I closed my eyes and took a deep breath, wanting to remember this moment, this feeling, forever.

"Addison Grace Smith," the principal called out.

I stood.

I looked back at my mom, eyes red with tears, and sitting in between my father, smiling proudly, and my aunt, looking almost sad.

I smiled at them, took a breath, and walked across the stage, accepting the diploma that most dreamers like me never get.

That moment was a dream come true.

I just hope the happiness lasts...

A year and a half earlier...

1

- Addison -
Thursday, December 1ˢᵗ, 2016

I woke with a start and tried to wriggle out of the covers on my bed.

"It's okay, just a bad dream," said the guy whose chest my head was resting on like it was a pillow.

"What time is it?" I burrowed into the covers further.

"About two."

I sat up and looked at him. "When'd you get here?"

"Sorry," Zach apologized. "After we watched the movie last night, I just didn't leave. I'm supposed to be staying with Billy, but he was up until two yesterday arguing with Cam over who should hang up first...and...when I came in here to grab my history notes, you were crying, and I didn't want to leave you like that," he admitted.

I smiled. "Well, thanks. Cam didn't seriously do that again, did she?"

He laughed, "It's not just Cam; Billy is just as bad."

We laughed for a minute or two, but then it was silent again. I couldn't help but think of my dream. It was too real. I shuddered a little bit.

"You ok?" Zach asked.

"Yeah. I'm fine. Just...cold that's all." He slid over until I was right next to him again. I leaned my head back on his shoulder. "I can't tell the difference."

"Huh?" He looked at me funny.

"I can't tell what's real and what's a dream anymore, not that I ever truly could. When people told me you were never real, I started to believe it myself, and now when I have dreams that you never came back, I wake up and you're here, but then my mind tells me that's the dream, having you here."

"Addison, I'm not leaving again," he reassured me.

"What about Mitch? Is he coming?"

"Well, yeah. He was mad I left him to come back here. But he thinks you don't remember anything. He isn't going to come after you, and if he ever does, I'm not going to let him hurt you. Not again."

"Zach?"

"Yeah, Ad?"

"I'm really tired," I admitted finally.

"But you don't want to dream?" he asked.

"No, I just don't want any bad dreams," I told him, and he kissed me sweetly. I was out cold seconds later.

* * *

I walked through the halls later that day lugging around a bunch of books that needed to be returned to teachers and papers that refused to stay in a neat pile.

School felt...different lately. I'm not sure what it was though. Dr. Hardy said it probably had something to do with the fact that I dreamt it already happened. She was also convinced that I met Zach at some summer camp years before and my subconscious just happened to remember him a few days before he showed up in town.

I feel like everyone thinks my "amnesia" is messing with me, and they treat me differently. Some people talk to me like I'm five. My friends include me, and they are trying their best, but you can tell they think I'm "off." Zach's the only one who truly knows. I think my parents want to believe me but don't know how when they are paying bills for MRIs for a brain injury I claim I never got.

Two hands covered my eyes just then as I opened my locker. I didn't panic because I recognized them right away.

"Guess who?"

"Tyler?" I guessed.

"Guess again," said the strong, deep voice.

"Billy?" I asked with a smile.

"Okay, you aren't seriously going to need twenty questions to guess who I am, are you?"

"No, not twenty. Just maybe one more."

"Okay fine. Guess who?" he asked me again.

"Zach?"

"Took ya long enough!" he released his hands from over my eyes and walked around to face me.

"Good morning, gorgeous," Zach greeted me with a kiss on the forehead and side-hug due to the massive stack of books cradled in my arms.

"Morning," I grinned back.

"Here, let me help you with those." He took the stack of books so I could unlock my locker.

"Thank you!" I walked up to my locker and swung it open. He stacked the books inside.

"How'd ya sleep?" he asked, which may sound like an odd question for a high school couple, but for us, it's completely normal.

"Great!"

"Liar."

"Hey! Were you in my head again? Don't ask questions like that if you already know the answer," I frowned up at him.

"Well, don't show me what's in your head and then lie," he jokingly argued back.

"I did not show you anything."

"Did too," he said, sounding like a child.

"When?"

"When you hugged me just now. You must have been thinking about it, so I saw it."

"Can't I turn this whole 'dream sharing thingy' off or something?"

"Nope. If you're thinkin' it, I see it."

"How can I make it stop?" I asked, closing my locker and turning toward him.

"No more physical contact," he said simply.

"Yeah...like that's gonna happen!" I laughed and walked into his open arms.

"That better not happen," he said with a smirk. I buried my head in his shoulder, breathing him in.

I turned my face to look up at him. "Hey, you still never explained how all of this works. You said you'd teach me," I told him. "Can't you like train me like Mitch trained you?"

"Soon, Ad," he said, avoiding eye-contact.

"You said that before. It's December, Zach."

"When it's safe, I will train you."

"But shouldn't you train me now? What if it's never safe? I should be prepared, right?" I asked and pulled away from him.

"I will, I just-" Zach was cut off by Cammie waltzing towards us.

"Hey, you two, I saw that PDA a second ago," she said in a very loud voice.

"What? It was just a hug," I tried to defend myself but was blushing a lot so I stopped talking.

"I know, I'm just messing with you!" She jokingly punched my shoulder, said she'd catch us later and started off in the direction of Billy's locker.

"Why did you stop talking when Cam came by?" I asked, turning to face Zach.

"Ad, we have to be careful who we talk about dreams around."

"Zach, I thought you told her? Jess knows."

"Well, Jess knows because she's Mitch's daughter, so she kinda can't get out of this situation, and I thought about telling Cam, but I never did."

"No, you told me you made her remember already."

"When did I say that?" He just looked at me.

"The other night. Right before Mitch came in my window."

"What?!" Zach yelled and pulled us more into a corner of the hallway. "When did Mitch come into this?"

"The other night before I woke up, and then you made me fall back asleep again."

Zach breathed a sigh of relief. "You were dreaming, Addison," he assured me.

It clicked in my head, and I remembered waking up next to Zach, so I must have been dreaming.

I got a weird feeling though that this wouldn't be the last time my dreams got jumbled up with reality.

* * *

"So," Dr. Hardy started, clicking her pen and turning to a fresh page in her leather-bound notebook. In a typical session with me, she filled up more than one full sheet of paper. "How are you?"

A seemingly simple question to which most people would say "Good. How about you?" But for me, in this setting, pen ready to write down my answer, I thought maybe Dr. Hardy was looking for an answer with a little more substance than "I'm fine."

I took a deep breath. "I'm alright, I guess. All things considered."

"So tell me what all has happened since our last visit," she said, finally looking up from her notes to look at me. But she didn't really look at me exactly. It was more like looking past me. It wigged me out.

"You mean two days ago?" I clarified.

She sighed, "Yes, Addison. What happened in the two days since I last saw you?"

"Same old, same old," I said. I didn't like how short I was with her sometimes. It's not her fault I'm in a therapist's office. It isn't her fault my dreams are this bad. It's not her fault my friends and family think I'm crazy.

"Addison," was all she said, while tilting her head a little to the side in a disappointed manner.

"Yes?"

"Tell me about your week." It wasn't a question this time; it was more of a command.

"Well, my week sucked."

She wrote that down. *Seriously? Does she have to write down everything I say and do?* I thought, growing more and more angry.

"And why is that?" she asked.

"Hmm, let's see! I barely ever sleep. I feel like I'm going crazy. My boyfriend is the only person on earth who seems to believe me, but then everyone else thinks I'm crazy for 'dating a boy I haven't known for very long'." I drew in a breath after that long-winded speech.

"Well, that would...suck," she said with a small smile, using my own adjective for the week, which annoyed me even more. "And how does that make you feel?"

How cliché, I thought.

I didn't answer. Instead, I swung my legs back and forth as I sat upright on the couch, looking around the grey room.

"I have an idea for you," she announced with a little too much excitement for the subject at hand.

"Okay?" I said warily.

"You seem to have anger and frustration built up from early this fall. You first came to me in early October. It's December. When asked how your current week is, you go back to the fall. I think we should address this so you can start to move on," she said, still not making eye contact.

Again, I said, "Okay?"

She finally looked me in the eyes, and I was struck (as I am every session) by how blue her eyes were. But they were dark at the same time. Like a storm cloud. They almost swirled, too, like there was a storm in her eyes. I couldn't look away, even though I wanted to. This lady could never usually look me in the eye, and it annoyed the crap out of me, but for some reason, the few times she would make eye contact - usually when she knew I wasn't telling the truth - I couldn't pull my gaze away from her. It was like her eyes were staring into me, finding the answers my mouth wouldn't tell.

"Great. So why don't you recap the past few months for me? Start back in late September. Briefly discuss the accident, coma, et cetera, then tell me briefly about what has happened up until now." She clicked her pen again, sat up straighter and leaned forward, eager to hear a story she's heard from me often - twice a week to be exact.

The storm cloud in her eyes swirled again.

Maybe she's right, I thought. *Maybe talking about of this will help. Maybe the more I talk, the better I will feel.*

So, I got comfy on the sofa (well, as comfy as possible because this couch was not the greatest) and took a deep breath, ready for my little tell-all with Dr. Hardy.

I sighed, "Alright, well..."

2

Friday, December 2nd, 2016

So, I sat there last night in Dr. Sandra M. Hardy's office and recapped the past couple months.

I started with the fact that three days of dreaming in a coma, to me, felt like a month. I woke up to find that October had never happened yet this year, meaning the guy of my dreams, Zach, never came to our small town. As far as my friends and family were concerned, Zachary Walker did not exist. He was a side effect of my amnesia and a figment of my imagination.

I have had strange dreams all my life, but doesn't everyone to some extent? I didn't think much of it. Until *It* showed up.

This creepy thing - man - was haunting me in my sleep, and I couldn't escape him. How do you avoid someone who's already in your head?

October came and went for me with the dreams reaching a whole new level of strange. I finally started seeing my life for what it really was: not normal.

But Zach always seemed to be there for me, even till the very end, outside of Pizza Palace when he told me he could make me forget it all, and the next thing I know I wake up in a hospital room with people telling me it's still September.

October never happened.

Fall Ball didn't happen.

I'm not dating Zach.

There is no Zach.

Which would, in turn, mean that there's no Mitch either.

"Who's Mitch?" they would ask.

Who's Mitch? My living nightmare. Mitch is evil personified. He is *It.* He stalked me for months on end, the dreams getting worse and worse and feeling more and more real each night. He told his nephew to pretend to fall in love with me as part of the plan.

It worked. His nephew is *my* Zach. I was so angry when I found that out. *They're related? That's just sick.* But Zach is more than his uncle could ever be. He's kind and protects me and is there for me when everyone else just wants to drug me again to make me stop saying crazy things. And let's face it - Zach is just downright *dreamy*!

Zach is just like me, Mitch, and Mitch's daughter/my ex-best friend, Jessica Clark. We are all dreamers. The best and the worst kind. Apparently, I'm special. Apparently, I dream different than anyone else in the world.

And that's why Mitch wants - no, *needs* - me.

He wanted to make sure I was like them, and when he found out how "special" I was, he decided to perform a little experiment.

A mysterious car accident happened right out front of Pizza Palace on September 27th, 2016. No one heard anything. No witnesses saw anything. From the supposed time I left my house, to the time Cammie's car veered off the road, no time had passed.

How did we end up there? How did Cam make it out without a scratch?

A young male called 911 saying a young girl hit her head when a car crashed into the side of his and she was now "having a seizure or something." When the local ambulance showed up, the EMT asked Cam what happened, and she couldn't remember a thing. Just driving and then *crash*.

For three days, I was in a coma due to head trauma.

During that three days is when I met Zach, in what I assume was some alternate universe or something. What else would explain him knowing who I was when he actually showed up a week later as the new kid at school?

Everyone stared as we stood in the hallway, the new kid calling me "Tour Guide" and me running up to him, jumping into his arms, and kissing him - something the quiet goody-goody Addison Smith would have never done to a stranger in a million years. Everyone said that was a side effect of my meds. Sudden personality changes.

But I know better. That time that I thought happened in real life may not have truly happened in the waking hours. But over the span of three days, I had the best and worst month of my life.

Then, after recovering from my supposed accident, I spent the next month reliving everything from my dream world. Little details would be off here and there, but for the most part, life happened almost exactly according to my dreams.

Am I psychic? Was it clairvoyance? I didn't know. But Zach, now here with me for real, said he can help me figure all this out. He's going to train me like his uncle trained him, so instead of my dreams being something negative, I can maybe use them for something good.

But I didn't tell Dr. Hardy that last part. No one can know that. They'd lock me up if they thought I still believed in an alternate dream realm.

I just don't know how I couldn't believe in it after everything that happened to me. Time seemed to move quickly in the dream world, quicker than in the waking life.

I wanted to know more about it.

I wanted to get stronger.

I wanted Mitch to be done with his little games.

I wanted Mitch to be done with me.

* * *

Friday morning I put a little more effort into getting ready for school. That was probably because I woke up super early and couldn't fall back asleep. I laid in my bed for hours until finally I decided I might as well get stuff done.

And I did! I organized some school papers, got some homework done I didn't finish the night before, made my bed (which I rarely do), read part of a book, did my makeup so I didn't look dead, and even had time to curl my hair.

When I got to my locker Friday morning, Zach smiled. "Hey, Ad!" he sang, grinning like an idiot and looked me up and down.

"Hi," I squeaked out. I've been with Zach for a while now, and sometimes I still can't talk around him. You'd think it would've gotten easier over time, but nope! I'm still the same old bashful Addison when it comes to this boy.

Every time he smiles at me I get butterflies. Actually, it's more than butterflies. "Butterflies" sounds like such a pretty word, but it isn't such a nice feeling. It's terrifying. This boy makes me so nervous sometimes just by smiling or calling me his "Tour Guide."

Tonight he's coming over for pizza and a movie. When we are together, I feel so much safer, like my dreams can't hurt me...at least for a little while.

"Soooo, how's Zach?!" Lily nudged me in the hallway on our way to lunch later that day.

"Good! How's Brad?" I nudged her back.

"What kind of a joke is that?" She stopped dead in the middle of the hallway.

"It's not a joke. You and Brad are dating again." I could feel myself getting defensive.

"No, we aren't! Why would you even say that right now? Geez! I was just teasing you about your boyfriend. You don't have to bring Brad into it." She turned and looked away.

"Oh, my gosh! Lily, I'm so sorry! I wasn't trying to tease you, honest. I seriously thought you two got back together when we were setting up for the dance."

"Cam was right," Lily said in a small voice. "You *have* changed." With that, she walked away.

"Changed?" I asked myself out loud.

That was one thing that changed from my dream: Brad and Lily didn't get back together. I kept forgetting that.

This is so confusing. Why can't my life be normal?

* * *

"Hello, Zach. Come on in," my mom said as I rushed down the fuzzy carpet staircase and then skidded to a stop by the front door.

"Thanks, Mrs. Smith," he said, and walked in.

"Pizza should be here in twenty minutes," she said with a smile, and walked into the office across from the kitchen. I looked in the doorway, and she was rummaging through sales papers and trying to find her readers.

"Soooo, what do ya wanna do?" I asked him while rocking on

my feet back and forth.

"Doesn't matter," he said, and kicked off his black and blue sneakers. "One question."

"Yep?" I looked at him in the middle of my entry way.

"How can you still look so pretty in sweatpants and a T-shirt?"

I blushed. "I don't know..."

He chuckled and walked up next to me. "Let's go pick a movie to watch after dinner."

"Okie dokie!" I agreed and headed towards the basement.

I walked up to the big brown suede couch and sank down into it. Zach came and sat next to me. I turned on the TV.

We started scrolling through the list of movies, but none really caught my eye at first. I kept pressing the side arrow button as a thought kept pressing on my mind.

"Hey, Zach?" I asked and looked up at his bright blue eyes.

"Yeah, Ad?" he said and looked at mine.

"Have I changed? Like a lot?"

"Changed?" He just looked at me.

"From when you first met me. Am I still the same Addison or not at all? Because people keep telling me I've changed and that my amnesia - or whatever they all think I have - made me a different person," I said, realizing now that what Lily said earlier affected me more than I thought.

"I don't know how much you've changed. You seem like the same, sweet, easy-going, beautiful, smart, awesome Addison you've always been," he said.

"Lately I just feel like everyone thinks something is wrong with me, and they don't know how to act around me." I scrolled through some more movies.

"I can change that, you know," he told me in a small voice.

"Huh?" I turned and looked at him.

"I can make you forget about your dream while you were in the coma. It was like you had one long lucid dream, but I can make it so that dream goes away."

"Bu-but then I wouldn't remember you," I looked at Zach.

"But your life would be normal again," he said and looked away.

"It wouldn't be normal without you in it," I told him.

"Well, I would be in it. I would still go to Madison High. I would just be the new kid who you don't have a past with."

"No! I don't want you to do that. I won't be able to forget you anyway, Zach."

"You'd think I was just some dream you had one time or you wouldn't even know me at all," he said as if it were that simple.

"How could you even say that? That would be a nightmare! 'Just some dream I had one time?' Why would you even-"

"Addison, it's okay. I won't do that to you...unless you want to forget." He grabbed my hands and held them tight in his. I hadn't even realized they were shaking until he steadied them.

"Well, I don't." I stood up to go upstairs for dinner.

"Are you sure?" he asked one last time.

I whirled back around. "Why would I want to forget you? Even if no one else believes me about my dream and thinks I'm insane, as long as you believe me and remember, then I don't care. That minute when I saw you in the hallway for the first time after the coma dream and realized that you knew me and remembered me," I shook my head. "I was *so* happy, Zach. You can't. You can't make me forget you. You're the only one who knows what really happened to me. You're the only one who can help me. And I-"

"Shhh." He jumped up from his seat on the couch and held my shoulders. "I'm not going anywhere if you don't want me to. And for the record, I couldn't make myself forget you even if I tried."

I smiled at him, instantly calming down. "Do you promise you won't do some weird dream vudu magic on me to make me forget you?"

"I promise, Ad."

He leaned in and kissed me just as my mom was coming down the steps saying dinner was ready.

"Pizza's here," my mom called down to us.

"Great!" Zach called back and started up the stairs.

I followed him up the stairs, but on the last step I felt dizzy. I paused for a second, then shook it off. *I seem to feel dizzy a lot lately,* I realized with a shudder.

3

- Mitch -

Friday, December 2ⁿᵈ, 2016

I stare myself down in the mirror in this small motel bathroom. Out of the corner of my eye, I see the blue light of the sign flicker and the dim words "no vacancy" crackle and pop as if the bulbs would burst any moment. No vacancy? Yeah, right. This dump is dead. Not a soul in sight. There is definitely a vacancy.

The only other losers here are Bill and the seventy-something, bottle-blonde Gladys who sits behind the check-in desk around the clock reading some trashy tabloid and obnoxiously popping her bubble gum. She seems like she couldn't care less if she got any business, which is good because there isn't any business to get in this kooky town. And that, my friend, is what makes it the perfect hideaway for a man on the run.

"Vending machine's almost empty," Bill calls from the room.

"Well, what do ya want me to do about it?" I bark.

"Stop eating so much!"

"Says who, ya big-"

"Big what, Mitch? Hmm?"

I just sit there. Then I hear the front door creek open.

"I'm taking a walk to the gas station for food. I'm sick of sitting in here with you."

"Fine," I say and pick up the plastic razor from the counter. He's such a whiney baby sometimes. He is the one who brought me here months ago with no plan whatsoever.

He says I am weak. But I would like to see him pull a stunt like I did. He thinks he is this master dreamer just because he can do a few things I cannot. Well, he is not the genius mastermind, I am.

I freaking convinced a teenage girl that a whole month happened in the span of three days. That stupid, tiny brat deserves to think she is crazy and get locked up somewhere. Yeah, let us just see who is the weak one.

I saw an opportunity, and I took it.

I have been in this girl's head for months, watching her dreams, analyzing her sleep patterns. I have been watching that whole crazy town actually, at least anyone in the town who is a dreamer like me.

But anyway, I had never pulled a stunt like that before. Just digging around in that idiot nephew of mine's head is exhausting.

Most people do not dream while in a coma, but in a few cases, patients have reported having one long dream, like watching an extended movie in their head during the length of the coma. And let us just say that most of those cases happen to be dreamers like me.

We are a rare breed, us dreamers. Some say it is a genetic defect that makes us dream the way we do, and in my case, have the power I have. But in my opinion, I say it is a genetic miracle rather than a defect.

Long story short, I knew Addison would be out cold in a coma for at least a few days. So, I got to work, plotting out this whole elaborate scheme. I made her think the whole month of October happened, starting with a trip to the mall that resulted in shards of glass, yellow tape, and her being interrogated by mall security. Then, my nephew Zach shows up and sweeps her off her feet. I throw some drama in there with my daughter Jessica - we will get to her later. Then, the perfect scenario, the school dance that every high school girl looks forward to. Madison High has been having Fall Ball since back when I went there. I know how excited the girls get over this lame night. So, I used that as the climax of the movie I had playing in Addison's head.

Then this girl wakes up in a hospital room *convinced* that it is the end of October and that her "dreamy" Zach will be there waiting for her. But when everyone around her keeps telling her none of that happened or there is no Zach or no Mitch, the poor girl thinks she is going insane.

Everything went according to plan.

I left Zach back at my apartment, all drugged up and sound asleep so his mind could be in Addison's dream while she was in her coma. Then I had Bill crash his car into Addison's friend's car, thus putting the whole plot in motion. Then, because her little mind is so fragile, I knew any head trauma would cause her to go into a coma.

Although, yes, I passed out after I worked my magic.

And, yes, Bill may have had to drag me away from the scene before the cops showed up.

And, sure, maybe I was still out cold when we showed up at this dumpy motel nine hours away.

And maybe it had been close to three months since "the incident" and I don't have another plan yet, but these things take time.

But, none of those things make me weak.

I am strong.

I just manipulated a girl's mind. I had her think she was in an alternate dream world for three whole days.

Who knows what is next for me? Maybe I'm closer to my goal than I thought.

You can do it, Mitch. You can do it.

I draw in a sharp breath. I nicked myself with this cheap razor.

A drop of blood trickles out of my pore, down my cheek, slowly, slowly, until it drips onto my fingertip.

That idiot Zach had to mess with my plan. Mess with me? His own uncle. Well, I am going to make him pay, make him suffer.

I will make him go crazy first. After all, I can be his worst nightmare. I am already inside his head. Same with the girl.

I stare down at the drop of blood.

I want to make him bleed. But maybe the best way to hurt him is to hurt her. So I will go after her.

A deadly snarl rises up out of my throat from somewhere deep within me.

Mess with me, you will be sorry. That is the lesson I have got to teach my kid nephew and those jerks from Madison High.

Look out, and sleep with one eye open there, Zachy.

4

- Mitch -

Sunday, December 4th, 2016

I sit there on the crummy bed in this dingy motel staring at the digital clock. The colon blinks once, twice, three times. I watch it blink fifty-seven more before the minute finally changes.

It is 11:11, and I know what that means.

Young, naive, little Addison waits for this time every night. Then she holds something blue --for God knows what reason -- and makes a wish. What an idiot. Like that would ever work.

I can see it in her mind though. She really believes in all that crap. She makes a wish -- most of the time involving Zachary -- and closes her eyes.

Last night she wished I would just go away. I don't think she realizes I can see all her thoughts.

I stare at the number on the clock, 11:11, glowing red in the dark of the room and concentrate.

I can see her now in my mind.

RODGERS

Eyes squeezed shut, she makes her wish. "Please
let me get a normal night's sleep tonight. I'm so
tired. Please," she begs.

I chuckle. Well, that just means I have to up the
ante tonight, does it not?

She looks almost back to normal after "the
accident": healthy, bruises healed. But her mind is
not. And that is where I come in. Her mind will never
be the same after what happened.

She opens her eyes and then looks up at a star in
the sky. She smiles at the star and then turns off the
light on her lamp. It is dark now. Finally.

She settles in for what she hopes will be a good
night's sleep and sweet dreams and all that crap. Her
eyes close, and almost instantly she's out.

It's show time.

I give her a minute or two of a typical dream,
let her think her little 11:11 trick worked.

Then, with a scrunch of my brow, she is
transported to a new place. A place so dark that you
cannot see. A place so hot that you are dripping with
sweat and feel like you are on fire.

"Where am I?" she asks in her quiet voice,
looking all around. "Zach?" she calls out.

Again, I have to laugh. *Right. Like he could save
you,* I think.

Her heartbeat quickens. Her eyes grow wide. She
is getting nervous. She knows I am coming.

I decide to shed some light on the subject and
open my eyes. They are typically the blue that is a
common trait of us dreamers. But I have acquired a
certain skill, and I like to use it to my advantage.
So, I let them glow.

Red light emits from my eyes, the only light in
this dark room. They glow brighter the closer I get to
her.

She must see the red glow because she whips
around to face me. "Please, no," she says, sounding
tired.

"Hello, Addison," I say in my most chilling tone.

"Mitch," she replies, trying to sound confident and confrontational -- two things she certainly is not.

"Have you thought about my offer?"

"I will never help you," she spits at me.

I narrow my glowing eyes at her. But she has learned at least a little bit. She will not look me in the eyes today. Finally the girl has caught on that looking in my eyes gives me control over her.

I try to step to the side right in front of her so that she has to look, but she turns away quickly.

"Fine," I say. "We will just have to do this the hard way. Again."

She shudders but does not run. (She tried that last time forgetting that in the dream realm things are different. She could run for miles, and I could just snap my fingers and pop up right in front of her.)

I grin at her through the dark. She grips her head, pulling at her hair like she can make the pain go away. I figured out this little trick during the dream days of her coma. She has such an intense power that I can use her own mind against her. I can make her think she is in an insane amount of pain if I focus enough.

Her knees buckle and she falls slightly. I reach out and catch her, then sit her down in the chair that happens to be there.

"You can do whatever you want to me; I won't help you," she says through gritted teeth.

"Yes, you will." I smile. *This will be too easy,* I think to myself.

I make the pain in her mind sharper, stronger. She cringes. I grin.

"Where is Carrie?" I ask.

"I don't know," she replies, sounding annoyed. *What right does she have to be annoyed with me?*

"Where is Carrie?" I ask again, my voice more demanding this time.

"I already told you: I don't know where she is."

"Do not lie to me," I warn with raising voice.

"I'm not lying! I don't know where she is. I haven't seen her in months."

I make the room brighter just by thinking about it. Now we are in my office. She is sitting in one of the chairs, and I am over by the desk. I look her in the eye for just a split second, and she shudders with the pain I can make her think she's having. It is my dream: I can do what I want.

"Alright, alright! She moved somewhere two hours from Madison, but I don't know where because she's never let us over there to visit. She always comes here."

Finally! Some real answers from the girl.

"How did she get rid of her dreams?" I ask, stepping closer and closer to her.

"How would I know that?"

"Addison," I warn.

"I don't know, alright! Don't you think if I knew that, I would've done the same thing to get rid of you?"

"Fine, then. Maybe Zach knows," I say with a smirk, wondering if she sees where this is going.

Suddenly Zach appears in the room with us. He looks around all scared and wimpy-like.

"Where am I?" he asks, even though Zach knows exactly where my office is and what it looks like.

But see, there's the difference. Zach is not really here. This is just my mind making it seem like he is here. He looks and seems real enough that Addison will believe it, but I will not hurt Zach in the process. Not yet anyway.

I have other plans for my nephew.

"Let's try this again," I suggest. I walk over and push on the pressure point in his neck so he squirms a little. I probably should not enjoy seeing that so much, should I?

She tries to leap from her chair to save him, but rope appears, tying her arms to the wood of the chair. "Zach!" she calls out.

He looks at her scared and wide-eyed and begs her to help. She fights against the ties.

"How did your aunt get rid of her dreams?"

"I don't know!" She sounds worried this time, flustered.

"Wrong answer," I tell her as I grab hold of his wrist and bend until it appears to be broken.

"No!" she screams.

"Try again," I order.

"Mitch, I swear I don't know. Let us go. I'll try to find out, but if you hurt us, you'll never know how she did it."

Obviously, I know this. Obviously, I will not hurt either of them physically...yet. This is a mental game. I will wear them out, make them think they're going crazy, until they cannot take it anymore and turn to me for help.

But right now she thinks this is real; she doesn't know this is all happening within the safety of the dream world. I have to make it believable.

I look at Zach. He disappears. Only his scream is audible after he has left.

"What did you do to him?" she screams.

"He's only getting in the way," I explain. "Bill will take care of him."

The sound of her terrified scream is the last thing I hear before she jolts awake, safe in her bed, wondering what just happened.

5

- Addison -
Monday, December 5th, 2016

I screamed and practically jumped out of my bed.

My heart was racing as I looked around my room. *What just happened,* I wondered. *Where's Zach?*

I shot out of bed and crossed the length of my room in record time, finding my phone sitting where I left it at my desk. I called his number as quick as possible.

Oh, my gosh, he isn't answering! I started to seriously panic. *What did Mitch do? What happened?*

I heard a click, hoping he answered. Instead, a voice said, "The number you have called is not available. Please leave a message after the tone."

No, no, no, no. Mitch came back for Zach! My mind was racing and jumping to conclusion after crazy conclusion, all of which featured Mitch torturing Zach somehow.

As the phone rang and rang, I tried to convince myself it had all been a dream. *No way Mitch would hurt his own nephew like that. Right?*

After about four incredibly long rings, he answered, "Hey, Ad," he said, sleep clouding his voice.

"*Zach?*" I asked, making sure it was really him, and he was really okay.

After a minute, he cleared his throat and sounded wide awake and worried when he asked, "What's wrong?"

I let out a breath I'd been holding since I pressed the button to call him.

"Ad?" he asked again. "What's wrong?"

"Nothing. Just a bad dream. I just..." I walked over and sat down on the edge of my bed, wiggling my toes in the shaggy rug. "I just had to hear your voice."

Now he was the one who let out a breath. "So, you're okay?"

"Yes, I'm okay."

"What was the dream about?"

I had to think for a minute. All of the anxiety I felt when I woke up clouded my mind. But, like always, the nightmare came rushing back into my mind.

"Well, Mitch was asking a lot of questions about my aunt and said he would hurt you if I didn't tell him. Then you were there, and I thought he hurt you."

"Did you know the answers to the questions?" he asked, sounding tired again.

"No," I admitted. "I wish I did, though."

"You'll figure it out, Ad. You're smart and you..."

He trailed off, obviously beginning to nod off again.

I smiled, sitting there alone in the dark. "Well, thanks, Zach. Goodnight."

"Mm-hmm," he mumbled. "G'night, Ad."

I couldn't help but smile as I pressed "end" on the phone call. I was just glad it had been a dream and he was okay.

I settled back into bed, curling my fingers around my bedspread and burrowing deep into my covers. I sighed in relief and tried not to think of the endless possibilities of tricks my mind could play on me this time when I fell asleep.

As long as Zach's okay, I'm okay, I thought and stared into the black.

A car drove down my street, and the light came in through my window and swept the length of my room. Then the light was gone, and I was left staring into the black again. I closed my eyes, and a small sliver of a smile spread across my face as I began to peacefully drift off.

"Zach won't be okay for long," a chilling voice sounds.

I snapped my eyes open and looked all around my room, straining to try to see anything in the dark.

But Mitch wasn't in my room.

He didn't have to be anywhere physically near me to hurt me.

He was already in my head.

And he was driving me absolutely crazy.

6

Tuesday, December 6ᵗʰ, 2016

"It's Tuesday, and you know what that means!" Señora Morgan cheered when Spanish class started the next morning.

"Tacos!" Jake called out.

She laughed, "Sí, Señor Jake, it is Taco Tuesday. I'm sure Señorita Glenda will be very happy you enjoy Taco Tuesday so much. But, does anyone else know what today is?"

"Term Tuesday," one student groaned from the corner of the room.

"Muy bíen!" Señora Morgan exclaimed.

Term Tuesday was something we had every week. We had to take a quiz on the vocabulary terms from the chapter we were currently on. Everyone dreaded it because we usually got the terms on Friday and had to have them all memorized (and spelled correctly, accent marks and all) by Tuesday.

"Noooooooooo!" Jake yelled, burying his head in the crook of his elbow on top of his stack of books.

"Silencío, Señor Jake. The sooner you get the quiz over with, the sooner you can get to lunch for tacos."

"You lie!" he accused. "Class will still be forty minutes."

"Es cierto," she conceded.

"I just want a taco," Jake whimpered to me as he turned in his seat to hand me the quizzes to pass backwards.

* * *

"Good afternoon, Addison. How are you today?" Dr. Hardy asked, not quite looking me in the eye.

As usual, that simple question annoyed me. I ground my teeth. Then I set my jaw, looked at her with my head tilted and arms crossed. "I'm fine."

"Alright." She scribbled furiously on her notepad.

Again I wondered how she already had so much to write down when all I'd said was "I'm fine."

"How have your dreams been?" she asked suddenly.

"Uh, no worse than usual," I told her.

"Could you describe a usual dream for me then?"

I thought about it for a second. I figured I had already broke down in front of this woman and essentially told her everything about my time in the dream world (or my coma as everyone else refers to that time period).

I told her. I talked about the most recent dream where Mitch tried torturing me and then Zach for information on my aunt, who I haven't seen in forever.

Why is Aunt Carrie such a big deal to this guy?

Dr. Hardy just nodded and took notes calmly. You'd think I was telling her a recipe or something unimportant.

"And how does that make you feel?"

"Not very good?" I asked, trying to figure out if this was the answer she was hoping for.

"Why?"

"Why? Seriously?" I took a deep, deep breath. *This lady!*

"Mm-hmm," she said.

"Well, it doesn't make me feel very good because this dude is still in my head. I thought that all would've ended when I woke up from the coma, but it's just gotten worse."

"And how so?"

"How so? He's stalking me in my mind. I can't focus. I'm terrified he's going to come back in real life this time. I'm worried he will hurt Zach too."

She seemed to almost laugh but quickly composed herself. *That was odd. It was like my answer pleased her. Or maybe her mind is somewhere else.*

"But that can't happen right? He can't actually hurt you in your waking hours, right? It's just your subconscious. Right?"

"I'm not so sure."

"Addison, I think you just need to relax a little. Let your guard down. You're just experiencing some post-traumatic stress."

"Relax a little? That's all you've got for me?" I asked her. *What kind of therapist is she?*

"It's normal, Addison. Just give it some time."

"This doesn't feel normal."

"It will in time." *If time is all it takes, why am I here? You aren't helping me!* I want to scream.

I stood and headed for the door when our session was over. She called over her shoulder that she'd see me in a few days. I wondered for just a second where Dr. Hardy got her degree. She just rubs me the wrong way. Annoys the crap out of me.

I told my mom after the last session that I wanted a new therapist. But because we live in such a stupid, small town, Dr. Hardy is the only one around. So I guess it's her or no one.

But then why do I seem to always tell her everything?

* * *

The doorbell rang and startled me in the too-quiet house that afternoon. *I hate being home alone,* I thought.

I leaned over on the couch, trying to get that perfect angle so I could see who was at the door without them seeing me. But I couldn't see who was there, so I slid down to the ground and crept toward the door. When I was little, I used to do this all the time, pretending I was a spy on a mission. Then as I got older, I did this after many warnings from my parents about not letting strangers into the house and all that.

But now, as an almost-seventeen-year-old girl, I still pretend I'm a spy and try not to make a sound or visible movement as I edge my way to the door. The threat has gotten real this past year. It's no longer a super secret spy or a robber who could be on the other side of that door -- it could be Mitch.

And to be honest, if it were Mitch, I don't know what I would do.

The bell rang again.

Maybe they'll just leave, I thought.

Suddenly, a voice sounded from the other side of the door. "Oh, Anne, for goodness sake, let me in!"

I smiled as I recognized who the voice belonged to. I jumped up and swung open the door.

"Aunt Carrie!" I squealed, and she dropped her bags and wrapped me in a hug.

7

"*S*weet Pea! Oh, I've missed my little buddy!" she sang, holding me tight.

"What are you doing here?" I asked, trying to recall the last time I had seen her-- probably last year some time.

"Just thought I'd stop and see my favorite niece!"

"I'm your only niece, Aunt Carrie," I said with a roll of my eye.

"I know! Aren't you lucky?" she asked smiling. "Where's your mother?"

"Pharmacy," I said, and she nodded like she already understood.

She clasped her hands together. "Now, help me get those other bags, will ya?"

"Sure! Does Mom know you're here?"

"Nope! And won't she be excited to come home and find me!"

I grinned but was thinking about how my mother is not one for surprises. Anything not in the schedule typically rocks the boat. My dreams and issues with that have basically made the boat capsize on her. Those were definitely not in her planner.

* * *

Later that afternoon, Aunt Carrie and I sat in the family room, curled up in the big reading chairs with mugs of hot cocoa.

"So, Addie, tell me about the boy from the pictures from that dance your mama sent me!" she said, leaning forward a little, ready for girl-talk time.

"That's Zach," I said with a smile.

"Ooo, Zach, that's a good name! Sounds cute! Is he?"

I laughed, trying to mask my blushing. "Yes, very."

"Score for Addie! Way to go, Sweet Pea! Do you have other pictures?" she asked.

I pulled out my phone and showed her a few we had taken on dates during the fall. She squealed with delight.

"My little Addie-pie is all grown up. She's got herself a boy now!"

I just took a sip of my cocoa.

"How long have you two been together?"

That question should have a very simple answer. But, for Zach and me, it's way more complicated than that. We've been going out since September, so that's about three months. But, we dated a whole month before that in my dreams, so, technically, that's four. But that's way too hard to explain to people.

"Uh, three months," I told her.

"Three months? Wow! Back in my day, most high school relationships lasted a date or two. But a few couples --the ones they call high school sweethearts -- stayed together almost all four years. But that was rare."

"Mom and Dad were highschool sweethearts, weren't they?" I asked, looking over to the framed photo of them on their wedding day that sits proudly on the mantle.

"Yes, ma'am! We all knew they'd get married. We were surprised they didn't get hitched on graduation day!" she laughed, then smiled warmly. "They just made sense together. Still do. They just...work."

I smiled back at her. I liked hearing stories about my parents when they were around my age. But it's crazy sometimes to think about if I got married at the same age as my mom, then I'd be getting married in two years!

"Ya know," my aunt's voice broke into my thoughts, "your Auntie Carrie had a high school sweetheart of her own!"

"Really?"

"Yeppers!" She stood up and picked up the now-empty mugs from the coffee table. "I'll go start washing these for your mum."

I followed her into the kitchen. "Wait, don't I get to hear about this guy?"

"Maybe another time," she said, turning on the sink, suddenly sounding as cold as the water rushing out of the faucet.

"But you just said you had a high school sweetheart. You brought it up. You've got to tell me now," I complained.

She turned off the water and turned to face me, drying her hands on a slightly tattered dish towel. "Well, it didn't end well, so I don't like to think about it, but we were going pretty strong for a few years back in the day."

She looked somewhere behind or above me, focusing on something else, the past maybe?

I stood there waiting for her to say something else. Finally she did, "Oh, Addie, he was perfect. We were perfect. We were the couple everyone thought would get married. He was the best looking guy in our class. I still have no clue why he picked me freshman year. We were inseparable. And I really did love him. I still don't know why I-"

"Why you what?" I took a step closer.

"Maybe a story for another day, hmm?"

My phone buzzed on the counter. She nodded toward it and smiled, "It's probably your high school sweetheart. Go answer it."

It was, in fact, Zach, so despite how weird that conversation went and how much I wanted answers from Aunt Carrie, I picked up my phone to answer. Aunt Carrie motioned she'd be upstairs and winked.

I smiled into the phone. "Hi," I said, the smile growing.

"Hi," he answered.

"Hi," I said yet again. *Wow, we have really turned into one of those couples, haven't we?*

He laughed. "So what are you up to?"

"Talking to you," I said stating the obvious like I usually do when he asks that. "Actually, guess what!"

"What?" he asked, and I could hear the worry creep into his voice.

"Aunt Carrie is here!"

"Really? Why?"

I couldn't help but sense the annoyance in his tone. "She's my aunt. Does she need a reason?"

"No, it's just she didn't do anything to help before. You guys barely see her."

"We see her every holiday," I pointed out. *Why was I getting so defensive?*

He took a deep breath. "Okay. Anyway, so she just showed up?"

"Yeah. But, Zach, let's be honest here, her only niece was in a coma, I think it's reasonable she comes to check on me. She's probably here because Mom knows I'm not better. I'm not an idiot. Everyone thinks I'm crazy. Of course it was time for Carrie to come."

"Ad, you aren't crazy."

"I know that, and you know that. But sometimes that's not enough, Zach."

"Well, if she wanted to help, why didn't she come when you were actually in the coma? Or a week later? It's December, Ad," he pointed out.

"I know...but I just want to have some fun with her. Like we used to. I want to forget all this for a bit."

"Right, sorry...okay so, I almost forgot why I called in the first place!" His voice changed for the last part, like he was forcing himself to lighten the mood.

"Right! Why did you call?" I asked, trying to fight back the smile that always seems to cross my face regardless of what this boy says.

"What are you doing this weekend?"

"I don't know. What am I doing this weekend?" I questioned, trying to sound coy.

"Well, I'm thinking we try Sal's..."

I shudder, remembering the dream from the "October that didn't technically happen." Zach and I went to Sal's on a date, and Mitch came after us. There were people screaming, me holding a knife, and Mitch with his glowing red eyes telling me Zach was his nephew. Then he let us go. He just let Zach carry me right out of that restaurant. He didn't follow us.

So that was one different thing between the dream world and my real life. When time rolled around for Fall Ball again, our date before that night was to a movie. I just couldn't walk back into Sal's again. I was too afraid that going there would cause Mitch to physically come back into my life, so we haven't gone back there since.

It was like Zach read my mind in the silence because he broke into it saying, "C'mon, Ad. No way that happens again. Don't you want some of those famous fries?"

Just the thought of the fries there made my mouth water. They were incredible. Sal was basically the world's best cook.

"Okay," I sighed. "Let's go to Sal's. I guess we can't avoid there forever."

"Well, we did go to Fall Ball and nothing bad happened," he pointed out.

"Very true," I said with a smile.

Fall Ball was actually perfect (the second time around). It was your typical high school homecoming dance, sparkly dresses, loud music, flowers and all. The dance was still masquerade themed like in my dream, but this time Mitch wasn't hiding behind one of the masks. He never came to the dance, there was no climactic scene with us fighting against him, and we never left the dance to go find Mitch and Jess. All that happened was that I got to dance with Zach and all my friends, and then we all went out for ice cream after. For once, I felt like a regular teenage girl living a regular teenage life.

But, of course, that feeling didn't last long.

8

- Mitch -

Tuesday, December 6th, 2016

Tonight Addison dreams of when she was young. More of a memory than a dream. A little seven-year-old girl running up to her favorite aunt. Her aunt, *my* Carrie, ruffles her hair and kisses her forehead. "I've missed ya, kiddo," Carrie says into Addison's hair.

"I missed you, too, Auntie Carrie! Are we going to go to the park today?" Addison asks.

In her dream, her aunt agrees to take her, and then in a flash they are pictured together at the big park in town. It is where everyone can be found on a hot summer day. But in her dream, it is fall, cold and brisk, and she and Carrie are the only ones there. Carrie pushes little Addison on the swing.

"Higher, higher!" Addison squeals.

"Are you going to touch the sky?" Carrie calls to her.

"Yes, Auntie Carrie! I can touch the sky!" She kicks her pink shoes up toward the clouds. She is nowhere near touching the sky, but Carrie congratulates her on touching it anyway.

"You're getting so big!" Carrie says with a sad smile.

"I know! Mommy says I'll be as big as her one day!"

"I'm sure you will. You're growing up so fast!" Carrie pushes her on the swing again.

"Did you have sweet dreams last night?" she asks.

Addison does not even bat an eye at this strange question. I do not question it either; I know Carrie well enough. She is trying to figure out if the dreams have started for little Addison yet.

"Yes!" Addison says happily. "I had a dream of puppies and bunnies."

"That sounds lovely," Carrie says. Her smile fades, and then she asks, "Do you usually dream of puppies and bunnies?"

"No."

"What do you usually dream about?"

The swing slows as Carrie forgets to keep pushing, too caught up in the question at hand.

"I dream about a lot of clowns. But not nice clowns or happy clowns. They are mean, and they try to hurt me or trick me." Addison still swings her feet back and forth and seems to still be content on the swing.

"Oh really?" Carrie asks. "Well, don't worry, honey. The mean clowns won't actually hurt you. I promise. If your dreams ever get too scary, you need to tell Aunt Carrie, all right?"

"All right," Addison agrees, still smiling. Then she counts to three and jumps off of the swing, landing with a happy squeal on the ground.

So now I sit there on the edge of the bed, trying to think about what Addison's dream means and how I can use it. But my mind keeps going back to Carrie, smiling and pushing Addison on the swing. That could have been the two of us, pushing our own kid on the swing. She told me she would always be there.

"Hey, Mitch, where're you going?" Bill calls out before I even realize I'm walking out the door.

I do not answer. I just shove open the door and walk down the hallway, past room after room. At the end of the hallway, I get to the iron steps covered in ratty old carpet meant to look like grass. Instead of going down, I climb. These stairs look like an old fire escape in the city.

I need an escape.

I keep going until I have reached the roof of the motel. I climb up onto it and walk across to the other side. I sit down and let my legs fall over the edge and just dangle there.

There is nothing holding me up here. It feels dangerous. I like it.

I cannot get that dream of Addison's out of my head. But it is not her dream I cannot shake, it is the image of Carrie.

"Did you have sweet dreams last night?" she had asked little Addison.

Just like she used to ask me. She would come bopping up to my locker each morning with that sly smile of hers and ask me if I had sweet dreams the night before. Typically, I said yes -- even though I most likely only had horrific nightmares of epic proportions -- because I would say anything when that girl smiled at me. If she said jump, I would jump. I would have done anything for her, and she knew that.

We could not talk about dreams much at school. Everyone on the team would rip me a new one if they found out that I talk to my girlfriend about my nightmares like I am talking to my mommy or something -- heck, the fact that I had horrendous nightmares was carte blanche to ridicule me forever. Guys just do not share feelings. Ever.

But some mornings, she would walk down the hallway with less confidence in her walk, her head hanging low, her eyes looking tired and dark. I knew what that meant. Her dreams the night before were bad. I wished I could help her. Her dreams were far worse than mine but not quite as bad as Meg's. On mornings like that I would walk up behind Carrie and wrap my arms around her, wishing I could block out the hurt.

"Talk later?" she would whisper, still in my arms.

"Of course," I would whisper back. "Always."

Sometimes kids would walk by us standing like that in the hallways and comment on how perfect we were together, "how cute". Carrie would laugh a sad laugh in my ear and whisper, "They have no idea."

People like to make assumptions based on what they see. They would see us together, standing there just hugging, and think we were perfect together. But what they did not know was that at night we were both tortured by our dreams. People said our lives were perfect, and in the waking hours maybe they were, but at night, while we slept, our lives were far from perfect.

They saw us win homecoming court or other stupid popularity contests year after year. They saw her as the captain of the cheerleaders, cheering on her boyfriend, basketball team captain. They did not see the girl who had to try so hard not to fall apart each day after not sleeping at all. They did not see the boy madly in love with the girl he met in his dreams the day before his freshman year of high school. They did not see the boy up at night because his dreams kept him awake, and so did his sister's screams as she dreamt of darkness, too.

No one in that school would ever realize just how perfect Carrie and I had been for each other. And the sad thing was, even Carrie must not have realized it either.

If she had, she wouldn't have done what she did.

9

- Addison -
Wednesday, December 7ᵗʰ, 2016

I heard someone scream.

I jumped up from my spot in the big, cozy chair in the front room and raced down the hall toward the back of the house where the noise came from. As I neared the family room though, I realized it wasn't a scream I had heard. It was just Aunt Carrie, who has quite the loud laugh sometimes.

I crept up toward the doorway to the family room and pressed myself against the doorframe, angling so they wouldn't see me.

The two of them were sitting on the floor in the center of our family room, Aunt Carrie falling over laughing so hard and my mother trying to compose herself, wiping away the tears that come anytime she truly, really laughs.

"Annie! What were you thinking with this hair?" Carrie squeals and shoves an old picture in front of my mother's face.

"Everyone had that hair then! It was the thing!" my mom argued back.

"But why did you curl it like that? God, it's awful!"

"Excuse me! You didn't have the best haircuts in the world, if I'm remembering correctly."

"Oh, Annie, you were always jealous of my hair," Aunt Carrie replied with a laugh.

"Oh yes, especially in that one picture you mailed Mom and Dad that one Christmas."

"Which one?" Carrie asked, no longer laughing, seemingly worried about her past hair choices.

"The cornrows!" my mom shouted, pointing an accusing finger at her younger sister.

"Oh, right," Carrie replied quietly.

"They had the little beads and everything! Where were you again?"

"I don't remember," she said, sounding genuinely unsure.

I craned my neck to see what was sitting on the floor between them. It was an old file folder box, the cardboard clearly falling apart on the edges.

"Would you look at this!" my mom cried, holding up a strip of photos from a photobooth.

"Aw," Aunt Carrie sang, leaning over to get a closer look. "That was your first kiss, wasn't it?"

My mom got this dreamy look about her as she stared at the row of pictures. I wished I could see them closer, look at each one, see what she looked like then.

"Bob was quite the romantic," she said with a smile. "We had just gone on a picnic, and then he took me to this photo booth that really only the younger kids went in. Then he just kissed me."

"The minute you came home that night I knew you two would be together," Aunt Carrie told her.

"How'd you know?"

"You couldn't wipe that smile off your face for hours -- no, days! Then you saw him again and that same smile was back."

"Oh right, like you didn't come waltzing down the hall super late at night with that same smile. I know you snuck out to see your guy!" my mom accused.

"What are you talking about?"

"Oh, come on, Carrie!"

Aunt Carrie, ignoring this, dug around in the box and pulled out a hand-painted mug that said "Best Sister in the World."

Then Mom reached in and squealed with delight. "Caroline Moore!"

"What?" Aunt Carrie looked up from the mug and then fell silent, her face shifting suddenly.

"You kept journals?" My mom pulled out journal after journal, all made of worn leather tied with ribbons to hold all the pages together.

"Where did you get those?" Aunt Carrie demanded. I took another step forward, itching to see what was inside that leather binding.

"In the box, Carrie, lighten up! I probably know everything in here anyway," Mom pointed out.

"Those are stupid. Just dumb poems and notes I wrote before. Not journals. Nothing important."

"I want to read it!"

Just as my mom began undoing the little bow, Aunt Carrie lept over the box and snatched the journals from my mom. "Just leave it, will you?"

I had never seen Carrie like that before. She was always so happy-go-lucky. Mom apparently hadn't seen this side of her often either.

"Oh, uh, all right. I'm gonna go get that wine now. I'll be right back." Carrie just sat there as her sister stood up and brushed her hands on her pants.

I ducked around the corner before my mom got to the doorway.

What does Aunt Carrie have in those journals?

I didn't know, but I had to find out.

* * *

"Goodnight, honey bee!" Aunt Carrie said as she kissed my forehead later that night.

"Goodnight, Aunt Carrie," I replied and walked halfway up the stairs. I peered back around the banister, and when I was sure she had gone into the guest room, I crept back down the stairs and into the family room.

The box was still there, but it had been pushed off to the side. When I lifted the lid, however, the journals weren't inside.

What did she do with them? I wondered.

I saw two white garbage bags standing by the door, waiting to be carried outside. Tomorrow was trash day. Smart. Aunt Carrie must've tossed the journals in here while my dad went to get the recyclable things. Luckily, he wasn't back yet, so I untied the one. Nothing.

I could hear heavy footsteps getting closer. Dad was coming. I quickly untied the other.

Bingo! There they all were, lying on the top. There were four of them. Small, leather journals. All the exact same except for the color of the ribbon tied around it. One blue, one yellow, one red, and one purple. I re-tied the garbage bag and ducked up the stairs, all four books tucked under my arm.

Once in my room, I sat cross-legged on top of my covers and fanned all four notebooks out in front of me. *Is there an order to these?* As blue was my favorite color, I decided to start by reading the one with the blue ribbon.

I glanced over at my alarm clock.

11:11.

Perfect. I squeezed my eyes shut, held the tiny blue ribbon, and prayed a silent prayer. *Please, please, let me find some answers in here. Please.*

Little did I know just how much I would find within these pages.

10

- Mitch -

Friday, December 5th, 1997

I don not know how, but I am in the past. I guess I was thinking about it and fell asleep. I am not sure how, but I am here now.

I look all around at the halls of Madison High back in its heyday; girls running around in their short little cheerleading uniforms because it was Friday, game day. God, I love game day.

Carrie comes running over to me. I close my locker door and look down at myself, a younger version of myself. I look like I did in high school.

Did I seriously just dream myself back here?

I realize with a shudder that that was what Addison was doing the other night in her dream without realizing it. She dreamt herself back to almost ten years earlier. If she had known what she was doing, she could use that to her advantage and start dreaming herself wherever she pleases. If she only knew the natural talent she had!

Carrie snaps me out of my thoughts by planting a kiss on me. "Morning, babe!" she says and steps back. "You okay?"

I nod, but she must not buy it. She leans closer and whispers, "Bad night?"

"You could say that," I tell her even though that is not the truth. The truth is that I am still adjusting to being back in 1997 in my high school junior body.

"You weren't at the tree house last night," she says, grabbing my hand and lacing her fingers through mine. God, I forgot how good that felt.

"Oh," I try to quickly think back to this day many years ago. *Why hadn't I gone to the tree house that night? What happened?*

I cannot remember, but before I can even give her some lame excuse, Bob, who was a friend of mine from the basketball team and dating Carrie's sister, Annie, comes up and claps me on the back. "DeMize, how's it hangin'?"

"Hey, Smitty!" I say and dive into our team's handshake. *How do I still remember that so many years later?* I wonder.

"What day is it?" he yells.

When I do not say anything he narrows his eyes at me and yells it louder. "What day is it, DeMize?"

I cannot help myself, I yell back, "GAME DAY!"

"That's right, brother, that's right!" and with that, he is off down the hallway toward class.

Carrie laughs, "You boys and your game."

I take a step back and look her up and down, taking in her tight cheerleading uniform I love so much. "Last time I checked, you love our game."

"No," she says, stepping closer to me, and I forget there are other people around us. I feel like we are in the dream world together.

"No?" I ask, a grin playing at the corner of my mouth.

"No," she explains, "I love basketball when *you* play it. I could care less otherwise."

Instead of answering, I just kiss her as the bell rings out above us, telling us to get to class, but we don't care.

* * *

I am standing in the locker room getting suited up for tonight's game.

"Hey, DeMize!" someone calls out. I turn my head in the direction of the sound. It is Bill. He is a buddy of mine, the point guard for the team. Not much of a basketball player to be honest, but his dad would have killed him if he did not make the team. I helped him find a position he could play, and we needed a point guard, so point guard it was.

"What's up?" I ask.

"Can you give me a ride home tonight? Car broke down."

"Again?" I ask.

"Okay, so not so much broke down as got crashed."

"You crashed the car again?" I stare at him incredulous. His family crashed cars like it was their job.

"Sandy did it!" he says way too defensive.

"Sandy crashed the new car?"

"Yeah, she fell asleep or something and drove into a telephone pole on the side of 75."

"Geez oh man, Bill. Is she okay?"

"Oh, yeah, she's fine. Car's not though."

I think about it for a second. "She just fell asleep?"

"Yeah, why?" he says giving me a funny look.

"That's just kind of weird, that's all."

I wonder if she's a dreamer, too, I remember thinking back then.

Coach yells for us to get ready, "Two minutes!"

We run out onto the court, music blaring from the new speakers. I miss this, I think.

The crowd is cheering, the announcer's voice comes out fuzzy over the dated speakers. I look over and see the home section filled up. Carrie stands at the front of the cheerleaders, jumping up and down and yelling some cheer. I can never tell what they're even saying when they cheer. She turns around and sees me. She winks and waves at me. I smile back.

* * *

Later that night I climb the rickety ladder up to the top. I try to open the old trap door without making too much noise. Mr. Moore is a light sleeper. I am always scared he will hear us out here and come out with the shotgun he likes to clean when I come to pick Carrie up.

I poke my head through the doorway.

She's already here. She beat me to it.

"Hey, baby," I say climbing in and closing the door behind me. I walk on my knees (this stupid old tree house is way too small for me) over to her and sit down cross legged across from her on the blanket she brought up here.

"Hi." She is beaming at me. I love that smile!

She leans across the small space between us to kiss me. "I love you, Mitch."

"I love you, too," I tell her.

She smiles and pulls out a small plastic grocery bag with a bag of potato chips, some soda, and bubblegum -- that girl always has bubblegum on her.

"Ya hungry?" she asks, cracking open a soda and taking a long sip.

"Nah, the team went out for wings after the game. All you can eat night," I explain.

"And did you?"

"Did I what?"

"Eat all you can eat?" she says with her twinkling little laugh.

I laugh, "And more!"

"Oh, Mitch, you didn't do that stupid contest again did you?" She pushes her light brownish- reddish hair back behind her ear.

This girl knows me too well. The team always has a contest of who could put away the most wings or slices of pizza or whatever we were having if we go out to eat after a win.

Carrie knows me best out of anyone. She knows the biggest thing about me, that I am a dreamer. Other than Carrie, only Meg knows about my dreams, and Meg is my sister. It was not until I knew that Carrie was the same as me that I felt I could tell her the truth.

It has been good though because we can help each other through it. Like tonight, while she took a nap up in the tree house and I held her while she slept. There is nothing I can do if her dreams haunt her tonight, but at least I can be there to tell her it will be okay when she wakes up.

I hope I can always be there to tell her that when she wakes up, I think, just as I myself wake up back on the roof of the motel, the sky above me completely black.

11

- Addison -
Thursday, December 8ᵗʰ, 2016

I couldn't wait to read the journals!

I opened it up and looked at the very first page of the one with the blue ribbon. It basically said "Annie Keep Out!" and had a bunch of doodles of flowers and hearts on the page. She also had written down a list of "dream meanings", like what it meant symbolically to dream of a dog or flowers or whatever she dreamed of.

I grabbed my little reading light from my nightstand, reached under my bed to where I hid Aunt Carrie's journal, right beneath the box spring.

I pulled it out and curled up in my covers, ducking under the blankets with my little flashlight, like a little kid reading past my bedtime. I run my fingers over the old, weathered leather. The soft and yellowed pages curling on the edges.

I sucked in a breath as I undid the ribbon tied around it to hold the stories inside.

I glanced at the very beginning of the first entry. December of her junior year, just like me. I wondered what types of things were going on in Aunt Carrie's life then. What if her life then is similar to mine now, with the dreams and all?

Dear Diary,

Today is Monday, December 1st, 1997.

I can't believe it is the first day of December already. Junior year has really been flying by! Annie thinks time is going slowly though. I think it is just because she is a senior and wants to graduate already.

I don't want to graduate though. I love it here at Madison High! When we graduate, we will all go our separate ways. And I don't know what my "way" is yet. I know I still have a year to decide, but I have no clue what I want to do with my life. That's probably because I can't stay focused long enough to think about my future.

I don't sleep much anymore. Dad says it's just insomnia. Mom knows better. This is far worse than insomnia. I wish I had insomnia.

Update: the dreams are getting worse. I don't want to go to sleep at night because I am so scared he will hurt me. I wish I knew who "he" was though. That would at least make this all a little better. I still have no idea who is stalking me like this. Or why. So I try to stay up as late as I can, reading, writing in this journal, or meeting Mitch.

I hope Mom never finds this diary! I don't know what I'd do if she found out I sneak out to see him almost every night. We have a system at this point. There's this little tree house in my backyard that my dad made for us years ago – well, he made it for Annie, but that's beside the point.

Anyway, no one ever goes there. Well, no one except us, I guess. If either of us can't sleep, we go hang out there around 1:00 in the morning. He lets me talk about my dreams and that always seems to help.

I think I'm going to go see him now. Goodnight!
Love,
Caroline

Aunt Carrie DATED Mitch?! I was so shocked I couldn't think for a minute. I needed time to process this, to breathe. *She used to sneak out to go see him? Did Mom know they dated? Was Mitch her high school sweetheart she talked about the other day?*

Oh. My. God.

My aunt dated my stalker, who is my boyfriend's uncle. This keeps getting weirder and weirder and weirder.

As much as I wanted to run down the hallway and go ask Aunt Carrie about all of this, I also wanted to keep reading. I only read one page and already learned so much about my aunt; there has to be more in here. So I turned the page and read on:

Dear Diary,

Today is Tuesday, December 2nd, 1997.

Last night was perfect! I met Mitch at night, and we talked and kissed and just laid there for hours in the little tree house.

Everyone knows about us in real life, but our dreaming life? It's a secret world only the two of us share. No one knows we both dream the same way. When my friends sigh and say we are perfect for each other, I just laugh because they have no idea. We are more alike than two people could be. We just make sense. And it makes me feel so happy to have someone I can tell all this dream stuff to who understands me. I know Mom says I can tell her, but this is different.

Mitch is the only one who knows how bad things have gotten for me. Things have gotten pretty bad in his dreams, too. He says his sister, Meg, she's a grade above us in class with Annie, has dreams far worse than either of us could ever imagine. I feel so bad when I see her in the hallways at school. She always looks so tired -- and paranoid, too, always looking over her shoulder.

So I love having Mitch there for me when the dreams get bad. Even to just have him hold me and say things will be okay. Apparently, he's read somewhere that there's tricks to this dreaming stuff. He says he will help me and that we can figure this all out together.

God, I love that boy! He couldn't be any better for me. Amazing AND a dreamer? I still can't believe he's mine. Sweet dreams (as if, right?),

Love,

Caroline

Not only did Aunt Carrie date Mitch, but she was *in love* with him?

12

I. Had. To. Read. More.

Dear Diary,

Today is Monday, December 8ᵗʰ, 1997.

Sorry I haven't written in a while; I've barely been getting any sleep. But when I do finally fall asleep, I have been having the strangest dreams lately. It all starts with someone chasing me. I can't escape him, and I run in circles with him close behind forever until finally I wake up. Then if I happen to fall back asleep it gets worse. I'm strapped into a chair in a cold room, watching someone in a hoodie torture my Mitch. They slit his wrists and punch him in the face until he goes unconscious. It's horrible. I scream and scream but they don't seem to hear me, or if they do, they don't care.

Last night, the person told him to kill me, and when he said no, the man in the hood pulled out a gun and pointed it at Mitch's head· I was shaking so hard· All I remember is screaming, and then I woke up on my floor instead of in my bed sweating, with tears flooding out of my eyes·

Who would ever hurt Mitch? He is literally the nicest guy in school, and everyone loves him· And who would want me dead?

I know it's all a dream or my hyperactive imagination or something, but I can't help but feel like it's real· What if there is someone out there who wants to hurt me? Or worse, hurt Mitch? He doesn't deserve to be hurt·

Love always,

Carrie

P·S· Mitch played so well in the game the other night· I was so caught up watching him play I forgot the words to one of the cheers· Coach Jen called me out for it in front of everyone· I was so embarrassed· But Mitch had a three-pointer, and I couldn't help but smile· The star player (who was only a junior and still the best player on the team) was all mine! Nightmares or not, I'm the luckiest girl at Madison High·

So those were the types of dreams Aunt Carrie had, I thought, turning the page to read on.

Dear Diary,

Today is Tuesday, December 9ᵗʰ, 1997·

Update: the weird dreams have gotten weirder· Now in my dreams Mitch is nowhere to be found· I run for miles looking for him but never find him· I go to his house, but his mother answers and is talking crazy talk. I can't understand her. I keep trying to ask where Mitch is, and she just says, "You're no good for Mitch. You're bad. You'll hurt him."

It's even weirder because Mrs. DeMize is one of the nicest ladies I know, always polite, put together, and smiling. She loves me, too! She always gives me a hug when I come over and sits and talks with me sometimes over tea. So why in my dream does she try to slam the door in my face and yell such crazy things at me? She sounds insane. That's when I know I'm dreaming; there's no way Mrs. DeMize would act that way in real life.

Then here is where it gets really weird; in the dream, on my way walking home from the DeMize's house, I run into this kid who goes to my school. His name is Ben, and he is in Annie's class. He's actually very cute, but I would never say that around Mitch. He's got light hair, and he's more of the tall and lanky kind of cute. He's the complete opposite of Mitch, come to think of it. Anyway, I bump into him on my way home, and we get to talking. Then we go get an ice cream cone, even though it is very cold in my dream. At the end of the dream I say I need to go home, and THEN··· He kisses me (and not on the cheek, I mean, like a real kiss!) and tells me he loves me, then vanishes into thin air.

Today in school I kept walking past Ben, even though I don't remember seeing him that often during school before today. Anyway, every time I would walk by, I would blush just thinking about how outrageous my dream was. I've never even spoken to the kid! Why would I dream he kissed me? Do you think it means something? Anyway, when I blush and walk by, he smiles· Then at the end of the day, when I walked by about the tenth time that day alone, he WINKED at me·

I didn't dare tell Mitch about it· He would have a cow! And, I mean, he only winked at me, right? So there's really nothing to tell· It's no big deal· I don't even know why I'm writing about it right now anyway· Oh well·

Goodnight Journal,

Carrie

Dear Diary,

Today is Thursday, December 11ᵗʰ, 1997·

Now in my dreams I'm dating Ben· Mitch is nowhere to be found, but I don't even look for him anymore· In real life, Ben is in my lunch period· (Mitch has class while I have lunch·) But I keep catching Ben looking at me, like staring· What is a cute senior boy doing staring at a junior girl like me?

I feel so confused· I want to talk to Ben; I feel drawn to him for some reason· And I feel like Mitch is already gone, even though he is usually right next to me· I've never kept secrets from him before, but what can I say? "Hey, Mitch, I've been having dreams that I'm dating someone else and I feel like I should give him a shot in real life, so let's take a break"? That's horrible! I hate the way this is all making me feel, the things all of this is making me do; the lying, sneaking around, having dreams about a guy who isn't my amazing boyfriend?

This isn't me·

Help!

-Carrie

I feel like the more I read her journal, the more questions I have about her life, my life, and Mitch's past life. I still can't comprehend a time when he wasn't a horrible human being trying to hurt me.

What does all of this mean? What happened? Does she pick Ben? Is that why Mitch hates me, like a second-hand hate that got passed down from her to me?

13

- Mitch -
Friday, December 12th, 1997

How did I do this yet again? I think, looking at the young kid staring back at me in the mirror. I glance around the locker room. *What day did I dream back to today?* I am in my jersey, so obviously it is a game day, probably a Friday.

"DeMize! Awesome game, dude!" one of the players calls to me as he walks out of the locker room.

"Thanks!" I call back, still unsure of which "awesome game" this was. I gather up my things and walk out into the hall where some of the opposing team's players stand, heads hanging low, all decked out in their Bulldogs jerseys.

Oh, now I remember! I think, realizing this was the night of the big upset. Everyone assumed the Bulldogs would crush us, but I had gotten quite a few three-pointers and soon enough we were well ahead. How could I have forgotten this game? It was one of the best games of my high school years!

Then it hit me, I forgot about that game because I blocked it from my memories.

It was far from the best night of my life. It was the first of a string of worst nights of my life.

My dream continued to play out this flashback. It was like watching a movie play out. Even if I told myself to go left, I went right, following the other guys. Walking up to the gym from the locker room to a thunderous chorus of "Good game!" and applause at the end of the night. If only they knew where this night was going…they surely wouldn't applaud that.

I forced a smile as people congratulated me, and this time ignored the fact that Carrie was nowhere to be seen. Seventeen-year-old-me did not know where she was at the time. But now I know. But I am going to save that story for later.

Some of us went out for pizza after the game, then to Bob's house to hang for a bit.

I ease open the back door at quarter past midnight, knowing my dad would be livid. I did not even call to say I would be late. Of course, I *knew* I should call, but I did not, and I could not change that this time around in my dream.

Would not have mattered if I had called anyway, I think as I look in the family room and find my mom out cold on the couch, just like she was the first time I lived this nightmare. I can smell the alcohol from here.

I tell Meg everytime this happens that Mom is trying to drown out the bad dreams. I know she has them too. I have heard her scream in the night. I have heard my dad's hushed whispers in the mornings telling her she is crazy. But Meg waves me away anytime I bring it up. "She only had a glass of wine or two," she says.

"Yeah," I tell her time and time again, "a glass of wine or two before she hit the hard stuff."

"Mom's fine," Meg says and walks away.

But tonight, I stand there, looking in at the mother who is more like a child at this point. The house is a mess, bottles everywhere, the smell of

alcohol a constant presence. I got used to growing up
in a house with candles always burning and some sort
of pie always baking in the oven. But now none of that
happens in this house.

Now I remember what comes next: a blood-curdling
scream.

Meg.

I run up the stairs.

"Let me go! Let me go!"

"It's all right, Meg, I'm here." I wrap my arms
around my older sister, but she kicks and screams even
more.

"Get out! Get out of my head!"

"Who? Who's in your head?" I ask. But of course
she cannot hear me. She does not even know I am here.
Her mind is in the dream world right now, and there is
no calming her down until this particular nightmare
ends.

Her eyes are squeezed tighter than I have ever
seen, and she is shaking like she is possessed or
something. Then, all of a sudden, she calms down.

I live in a family of psychos! I say to myself,
and ease my sister's head back onto her pillow. I wait
until I am sure she is fully back asleep.

I walk back to my room, knowing full well what is
coming next.

Tonight is the first of many nights I will stay
up waiting for my dad to get home while my mother and
sister suffer terrible nightmares. The only benefit is
that at least for a while, I do not have to go to
sleep and deal with my own nightmares.

My dad comes in the door at 3:15 in the morning.

"Where've you been?" I ask.

"Go to bed, Mitch. It's late," he mutters,
walking away.

Yeah, I know it's late.

I walk upstairs and get ready for bed. Tonight's
dreams are gonna suck. I remember that much.

14

- Addison -
Friday, December 9th, 2016

I woke up early Friday morning -- couldn't sleep *again*. But even though it was roughly three in the morning, my stomach growled, very loudly. So I got out of bed, but the cold December air was sharp and made me shiver. I grabbed the fuzziest robe I owned and my bunny slippers. I got the slippers a few years ago, and they are huge and honestly kind of creepy looking, but they are so warm I could never get rid of them.

I went downstairs as quietly as I could, careful not to wake up the rest of the house. Aunt Carrie was asleep on the couch, and Mom says she's a light sleeper. So I grabbed a granola bar that was sitting on the counter and crept back up to my room, easing the door closed carefully and trying to quietly open the wrapper of the granola bar.

I sat there on the edge of my bed for a few minutes just thinking about what all of Carrie's journals mean. She started dreaming about another guy, but was she really falling for him? And

Mitch sounded so different back then. He sounded like a normal guy, not some psycho-dream-stalker like he is now.

I wonder what happened.

* * *

I rushed down the stairs when I heard the doorbell ring later that morning. I swung it open to see his smiling face.

"Happy Birthday, beautiful!" Zach whispered in my ear, then gave me a quick kiss on the cheek.

"Thank you," I told him, smiling and stepping aside so he could come in.

He handed me a card with blue flowers and blue balloons on the front. "Happy Birthday to the Best Girlfriend in the World!" it read.

My dad came rushing down the stairs, obviously running late for work. "Happy Birthday, sweetheart!" he said, kissing my forehead while tying his dark blue tie.

"Thanks, Dad," I said as a loud noise came from the kitchen. My dad and I just looked at each other, eyes wide. I set the card down by my things, and we both turned and headed toward the kitchen.

"What's going on in here?" he half-yelled, half-laughed, taking in the sight of pots and pans scattered around the floor, boxes and recipe books crowding the counter, and Aunt Carrie kneeling on the countertop, reaching for something on the very top shelf of the cabinet. A bag of flour tipped over the edge of the cabinet, pouring out all over the floor.

"Oh, hey, Bob. Nice tie," she said simply.

Zach chuckled behind me.

"Carrie, what is all of this?" my father asked, glancing down at his watch.

"I can't tell you. Addie is standing right there," she told him in that voice when you're trying to be secretive and sly and it just isn't working.

"Whatever, I'm late for work." He turned to me, "Have a great day, Addison!"

"You too, Dad!" I gave him a hug and handed him his traveller's coffee mug that was on the island next to me.

He nodded as he took it and rushed out the door.

Carrie climbed down off the island and brushed the flour from her bellbottoms. "You must be the famous Zach! It's so great to

finally meet you!" She grabbed him and pulled him into a big hug --
Aunt Carrie was quite the friendly one.

"Oh, uh, hi," he said, looking at me over her shoulder. I just
smiled.

"So," she said stepping back, "I hear you're relatively new to
town. How do you like it here?"

"It's great! My mom grew up here, so it's cool to see some of
the places she used to talk about."

"Your mom? It's a small town. I'm sure I know her. What's
her name?" she asked, leaning back against the now-messy
countertop.

"Meg DeMize," he said. I realized I'd never heard Zach's
mom's last name before. *That's a strange last name,* I thought, *it
sounds like "demise".*

"DeMize?" Aunt Carrie asked, standing up straight. She
looked nervous or upset all of a sudden.

"Yeah, did you know her?" Zach asked, in a tone that made
me think he knew more than he was letting on.

"Uh," Aunt Carrie faltered, which was unsettling because she
always knew what to say and never missed a beat.

"Did you know her, Aunt Carrie?" I asked, tilting my head
and just staring at my aunt. After reading her journal, I knew she knew
who Zach's mom was. But, of course, I couldn't tell her I knew that.

"Uh, yeah, I did. She was in your mom and dad's class. A
grade above me."

"Oh, well, then you must've known my uncle too," Zach
pointed out, again with that weird tone to his voice.

I thought about how at the dream Fall Ball Mitch asked if I
was related to Carrie. I figured then that they knew each other, but
now knowing they were in love? So weird.

"Your uncle?" she clarified.

"Yes. His name is Mitch. He would've been in your class,"
Zach said, standing up a little straighter, a more...dominant stance.

"Oh, Mitch, yeah. I knew Mitch. We had some classes
together, I think."

Liar, I thought.

Zach just kind of nodded, almost waiting for her to say more.

"Well, I better go find the broom to clean this mess up, and you two best be getting off to school, hmm?" She gave me a quick hug as she headed down the hallway.

I turned to Zach. "What was that all about?"

"What was what all about?" he asked, starting to walk down the main hallway toward the front door.

"That," I said, because I wanted to know what he knew.

He reached down and picked up my backpack, handing it to me as I pulled my jacket on. "We're going to be late," he said.

"Why are you avoiding the question?"

"I'm not; we are just going to be late, that's all." He swung open the front door and gestured for me to go first. "Birthday girl first!" he said, suddenly sounding chipper again.

Soon we were walking hand in hand into school.

"Did you start writing that paper yet?" I asked him as we rounded the corner of the hallway.

"Addison," he said with a nod of his head in the direction of our lockers.

"What?" I looked over that way.

"Cam!" I squealed taking in the ginormous bow plastered on my locker. It was bright blue and huge, and glitter was falling from it all over the floor in front of my locker. It looked like one of those giant bows you get to put on a car for a girl's sixteenth birthday or something.

"Happy Birthday!" someone called over their shoulder as they walked by. I don't even think they knew who I was. But I guess if I saw a bow like that, I would have acknowledged it too.

"Get over here, birthday girl!" Cammie hollered.

I rushed over into her open arms. "Happy B-day, kiddo!" She pulled back and pretended to examine my face. "Seventeen. Wow! You're so old!"

Zach placed a hand on my back, "I'll see ya in class, Ad."

"Bye," I said and reached out and squeezed his hand, then I turned to Cammie. "I am *loving* this bow!"

She winked then, "I saw it and thought 'If this doesn't just scream Addison Smith's birthday, I don't know what will', so I bought it."

"And I love you for that!" I told her.

"So did your mama do that thing where she wakes you up at exactly the time you were born to sing to you again?"

"Yes!" I said laughing. My mom has done that for as long as I can remember.

"5:18 a.m., like clockwork every year."

"Oh, yes! Never a second late."

"Gotta love your mom!" Cammie said as we walked into the room for our first class today.

Today. The 9th of December. My birthday. You know what I'm going to wish for this year? Just one good night's sleep. And answers.

I could really use some answers.

15

*L*ater that day I was sitting in study hall clicking my pen cap. Up and down. Click, click, click, click, click.

I was getting edgy. I wanted to read more of that journal.

I know I shouldn't have brought them with me here to school, but I didn't want my mom or Aunt Carrie to find them in my room today. Also, I really just wanted to know what happened next, so I shoved them in my backpack as I was getting ready today.

"You okay?" Zach asked.

"What? Oh, yeah, I'm fine." I said, wondering why he would ask. Then I thought to myself, *Obviously he could hear your pen clicking again and again, Addison.*

He stood up, giving me a look that I knew meant he'd ask me if I was okay again later today. "Okay, well, I've gotta go get a form from the office."

"Okay!" I said, as he kissed the top of my head and left. The minute he left the room, I pulled the journal tied with the little blue string out from my backpack. I looked all around, just to be sure no one (like Mitch) was looming over my shoulder.

I went to the page I left off on, and I read.

Dear Diary,

December 12th, 1997

Last night I dreamt Mitch was trying to hurt me. But then all of a sudden the table literally turned, and I was the one standing over him, and he was the one cowering in fear. It was the first time I dreamt of Mitch in a while.

Yesterday Mitch asked me how my dreams were as we laid together up in the tree house. Typically, I tell him the truth. And usually, he is somewhere in my dreams. But how could I tell him I barely dream of him anymore? That sounds really bad, don't ya think? And what is even worse is that I've been dreaming of Ben. To some people that doesn't matter, "it's just a dream," but for people like Mitch and me, who are connected by dreams, dreaming of another guy means a heck of a lot.

What am I going to do?

Carrie

Dear Diary,

Dec. 17th, 1997

Today I just couldn't help it. I don't know what came over me. I slipped a note in Ben's locker (it happens to be a few down from Annie's) and when I was talking to her this afternoon, I noticed him go in his locker and find the note. He looked up and nodded at me. The note told him to meet me under the bleachers at the next basketball game.

What was I thinking? I'm not an "under the bleachers" kind of girl! I don't do that! I've never even met Mitch under the bleachers. The treehouse has always been our spot, and think of how innocent and young a tree house sounds.

I honestly think I'm going insane· "Meet me under the
bleachers· Friday· 2nd quarter· -C"

I signed it "C", not even "Carrie"? That isn't me· Mitch
will die if he ever finds all of this out·

-Carrie

None of this sounds like the Aunt Carrie I know. What
happened to her?

Dec· 19, 1997

What is wrong with me? I have an amazing boyfriend
who loves me and cares about me, and I go and act like an
idiot!

Tonight was a big home game· I watched and cheered
for the team· I cheered on Mitch and winked and waved when
he looked my way as usual· But during the second quarter, I
said I had to go to the bathroom, and when I was sure no
one was looking, I slipped under the bleachers· Ben was
standing there, waiting for me· He said he didn't think I
would show and had hoped the note was from me· He told me
he doesn't usually "go with girls that are younger" than him,
but that I'd be an exception· I have to admit I had butterflies
in my stomach the whole time I was talking to him·

We talked for about five minutes before he just kissed
me· We made out under the bleachers until the buzzer
sounded for halftime, and I ran away because I couldn't believe
what I had just done·

I'm a terrible person! I just don't know what it is
about him· I feel like I'm meant to be with Ben, and I can't
seem to help the way I feel around him· He said to call

tonight if I wanted to. And Mitch said to meet him in the tree house tonight. I haven't decided what to do yet.
What have I done?
-Carrie

"Whatcha reading?" Zach's voice startled me and jolted me back from 1997 to the present.

"Oh, uh, just a book."

"All right?" he said questioningly. "What kind of book?"

"Well, it's, uh-" I didn't know if this was something I could tell him. What would he think about me reading Carrie's journals? I mean, it's kind of silly, spending my time reading my aunt's daily thoughts like this. I just know there are answers inside these journals.

"Are you not sure?" he asked, bringing my mind back to the present. "Is the book that bad?"

"It's nonfiction," I blurt out.

"You read nonfiction?" he questions with a chuckle.

Why is that so hard to believe? "Yes, it's my favorite type of book to read," I huffed.

"Oh, please! You're favorite books are those sappy, romantic, happily-ever-after, guy-finally-gets-the-girl books." He pulled back a chair and plopped down in it next to me. He put his elbows on the table and propped his chin on his fist, then flashed me that signature Zachary Walker grin.

"So you like nonfiction?" he asked.

"As a matter of fact, I do. It's interesting."

He smiled, and his eyes showed a flash of something - playfulness? Disbelief? "My girlfriend is *such* a nerd!"

"Hey! You're lucky you-"

He cut me off in the best way, kissing me mid-sentence, making it so I just have no choice but to kiss him back and consequently forget what I was saying. He always does that when he's teasing me and knows I'm about to start rambling.

He pulled away and leaned back in his chair. "Nah, I like when you get all nerdy. It's cute."

"My boyfriend is *such* a sappy, romantic guy!" I teased.

We sat in the library studying until the bell rang and we had to leave for lunch. As we were walking out into the hall, he was talking about some war movie that Jake wants to go see with him. But I was thinking about back in study hall. *Why did I hide the journals from him? Why didn't I just tell him?*

I looked up at Zach who I think was still talking about the movie, "...but now Jake is talking to this girl, and there's a chance she wants to hang Friday, so we probably won't go see it--"

"Zach?"

He almost stopped walking, always worried I'm going to tell him Mitch is there or something. "Yeah?"

"I lied."

"Huh?"

"Well, I didn't *lie*-lie. I just didn't tell you the truth. I just kind of --I don't know. I'm sorry."

"Ad, what is it?" He steered me out of the traffic of Madison High hallways over to the side by the lockers that are always empty.

"The book I was reading. Well, I do read non-fiction sometimes, but that wasn't. I mean, I guess it is. It isn't made up." I shook my head, *Get to the point, Addison!*

"Ad?" Zach just looked confused.

"I've been reading my Aunt Carrie's journals!" I blurted.

"Okay? What does that mean exactly?"

"It means I found -- well, I stole them out of the garbage when she was asleep. But if they were in the garbage, then it's not really stealing. Anyway, I have her old journals from back when she was our age and dating your uncle, and they're all about her dreams and her life then. I'm trying to find out what happened to her."

"So what did happen? How did she get rid of the dreams?" he asked, looking very interested now.

"Well, I don't know that yet. But I feel like these journals could have some real answers in them. It's so crazy though. Mitch sounds like a completely different person back then. So does she though. I feel like I don't even know the girl I'm reading about."

"That's crazy. Sometimes I still can't believe those two were a thing."

"Right? It's so weird. My aunt and your uncle." I tried to shake the thought away.

Zach didn't say anything then, he just kind of stood there, looking past me at the endless stream of students rushing to class.

"I'm sorry I didn't tell you," I told him.

He finally looked me in the eye, "You did now. It's fine." He paused, took a breath, then stood up straighter and asked, "Can I read it?"

Can he read it? My aunt's journal? "Uh, sure. I'm almost done with the December one. You can read it when I'm done."

He started walking again. "Sweet! I need some answers too. Maybe they'll be in there."

"Yeah, maybe."

I really hope so.

16
- Mitch -
Friday, December 9th, 2016

"So, give me the down-low," Bill calls, waltzing through the front door of the motel room after disappearing for twenty-four hours.

"Where the hell have you been?"

"Out."

"Out?" I growl. This guy is really beginning to tick me off. You can think someone is an easy-going person and all, but when you are suddenly trapped in a small motel room, their true, annoying colors really show.

"Yeah, out. What's it to ya?" He flops back onto one of the beds and kicks off his shoes.

"You said you were going out for food."

"Yeah?"

"That was yesterday, Bill! You didn't bring back any food. I'm hungry," I complain.

"I did get food," Bill tells me while he gets all comfortable like he's about to go to sleep.

"Where is it?"

"I ate it on the trip back." He yawns.

"Back from where, Bill?" I ask through gritted teeth. Would it be bad if I killed him right now?

"Madison."

"Why did you go back home?" Okay, now I am mad. The guy leaves, saying he's off to get food, and comes back a day later from the town he said we had to leave.

"I had to talk to Sandy."

"Pick up a phone then. Why would you risk going there?"

He sits up, takes an angry breath, and looks me dead in the eye. "Might I remind you that you are the one who needs to hide, Mitch. Not me. I have done nothing but help you."

"And eat all the food," I grumble.

"I had to go see her, Mitch. She's my sister. Her dreams are intense, and she keeps taking these pills...I don't know, but she's a mess. I don't want to see her end up like-"

"Like who?" Then it dawns on me. "Like Meg? That wasn't my fault. I tried to help her."

"Mitch, if Meg would've just let Sandy help her, she could've-"

"Let Sandy help her? You mean the mental psychiatrist? Oh, yeah, what a great option. Sandy definitely would've helped Meg. You're right. Maybe she could've prescribed her some of those pills, huh?"

"You know what, Mitch? I'm sick of this shit," he yells, standing up and running his hand through his thinning hair.

"Then leave," I bark.

"I can't."

"Why not?" He should just leave. He is such an idiot. I do not need him. He is only holding me back.

"Because I talked to Sandy. She said Addison's sessions are getting close."

"Close to what?" I ask.

"Close to where you want the girl. Soon Sandy can get more in her head. The girl tells her stuff. I mean, you know, you've seen Sandy do that weird eye-

vudu crap. She's got Addison believing she can trust
her. We need to figure something out. We need to get
to Addison before she realizes just how much power she
has."

Crap.

***

I cannot sleep. I mean, I rarely do sleep, but
still, tonight, I cannot even rest at all. I need
somewhere to think. I get out of the bed and go back
to the rooftop. The cold air smacks me in the face as
soon as I step on the roof, but it feels good. It
energizes me.

*What am I going to do about Addison? If she
realizes all that she can do within the dream realm,
she will be unstoppable. If I could just convince her
to work with me and my team...*

I shake my head. That will never happen with Zach
around her. They cannot be together. I need to split
them up. It is for their own good. And mine.

I look up and concentrate on one star in the
black sky. The light grows bigger, brighter, until it
fills my entire vision. I can feel my pupils dilating,
adjusting to the light, adjusting to the shift in
worlds.

Now I am in a dream. Zach is there too. It is
back on the night of Addison's "coma dream" with the
giant rock over the trap door into my lair. I let
Addison go after that, let her live her daily life
covered in bruises and aches to remind her of my power
over her in her nightmares. But I kept Zach in the
dream realm for the next few days. This was right
before Addison dreamt herself to Zach to "save him".

She is such a hopeless romantic. It annoys me. No
love story has a happy ending. Trust me.

Anyway, tonight I am making Zach relive that
dream while he sleeps.

"Zach," I start. He looks away angry.

"You can do whatever you want to me. But leave
her alone."

"Zach, I need you to take Addison out of the
picture."

72

"What? No." He tried to stand up, leave maybe, but he cannot. He is too weak. I have only given him the bare amount of food and water he needs to stay alive. I need him alive.

"Zach, you knew the plan all along," I point out.

"No, I really didn't. You barely told me anything."

"You were supposed to distract her, just a little. Get me some information. Then break her heart. She still seems infatuated with you, my boy."

"I can't."

"Yes, you can. At this point it would be pretty easy." I walk up closer to him. "Have her catch you with Jessica, or better yet, her best friend, what's her name? Callie? Candy? Either one, it's a sure-fire way."

"I'm not going to do that, Mitch."

"Don't tell me you have feelings for that girl," I tease.

He just sits there, looking at the ground.

"Zachary!" I crouch down right in front of him, levelling my eyes. "I have worked too hard and too long for you to mess up my plans for some girl. She already knows too much. My plan will not be taken over by a no-good, low-life kid like you. I won't have it. If you don't break that girl's heart soon, I will. I swear, I will break her."

"Mitch," he pleads.

"Shut up. I've given you everything, raised you when your daddy bailed, taught you all I know and gave you a good life. You will not throw our lives away for some girl. I won't have it."

"Uncle Mitch…"

I stand up and turn to leave.

"Uncle Mitch, where are you going?"

"To make your girlfriend's life a living hell."

He tries to get up, tries to somehow fight back, but he cannot. So weak. It is a shame. He could have been a good dreamer, but he has too big a heart. It will only get in the way of things.

17

- Mitch -
Saturday, December 13th, 1997

I feel someone move next to me. I wake up, realizing I must be back in 1997 again. I look down and see Carrie laying with me. She sees me and seems to force a smile. She squirms closer to me until I do not think she can get any closer.

"Hey, baby," she says sounding tired. "How did you sleep?"

I guess I had not realized that I slept without any dreams until she asked. "Fine," I tell her.

"Good," she says in that voice she uses when she wants something. "I've missed you," she lies.

Really? You are the one who has been avoiding me, and I have no clue why. (Of course, now that it isn't 1997 anymore, I know why, but in reliving my dream from back then, I do not.)

"You've been busy," I reply automatically.

"I have! But I'm sorry. I'll make more time for us from now on, okay?" Her second lie that night.

"Okay."

"Mitch? Are you mad at me?" she asks while she gets even closer to me. She is obviously playing some game right now, but how am I supposed to think straight while she is this close to me?

"No. Why would I be mad at you?" I ask, trying to focus.

"Just checking."

She looks around the tree house then back at me. "Wanna make out?" she asks suddenly.

I know I should leave. I know what happens later, who she goes to see after she leaves here. But back then I still had hope that everything was fine between us.

Can I change what happens when I dream back to the past? I wonder. But I know that I cannot. There is no way to change the past. I am just reliving my life in a series of memories in my dreams.

Oh, what the hell, I decide, and lean down, letting her think she can make this situation better with her wild kisses. I should get something out of this nightmare.

* * *

"Hello?" I say into the telephone the next day.

"Hello?" a woman's voice replies. "Mike? It's me."

"Sorry, who is this?"

"Michael, come on," she says in a teasing voice.

"This isn't Michael," I say.

"Oh, I'm so sorry!" She sounds flustered and confused.

"Do you want me to leave a message?" I ask, trying to figure out what woman would be calling my father.

"Oh, uh, no, thank you."

Click.

* * *

Two a.m. and I am still awake. I keep thinking about that woman who called earlier. Who would be calling to talk to my dad? Who would be calling him without knowing who I am?

My mom's screaming brings me back to the present -- well, the past, because I am still stuck in 1997-- and I climb out of bed and drag myself down the hall where I find her passed out in the middle of the hallway, dangerously close to the stairs.

"Mom, wake up. Snap out of it," I say for the millionth time in my life, and prod her shoulder.

She startles awake. "What is it, Mitchell?" she asks through sleepy eyes and a foggy mind.

"Nothing, Mom. Are you okay?" I ask.

"Yes, sweetie. Go back to bed," she says as if I am the crazy one who woke up with a nightmare. You cannot have nightmares if you never fall asleep in the first place -- at least, that is how I look at it.

She curls up against the railing, cozying up like it is totally normal to sleep in your hallway. I sit against the wall and curl my knees up to my chest. I sit there watching her for a minute to make sure she is breathing and to kill some time.

When the front door eases open, I am just starting to nod off. Then my dad comes clambering up the stairs. "Get to bed, Mitch," he barks when he notices me from the bottom of the steps.

I stand to leave, not wanting to get in a fight with an obviously-wasted dad. That is when he notices my mom laying there, sleeping soundly for the first time this week. "Psychotic woman," he mutters (along with a string of other words) as he steps over her body and walks into their bedroom. The door closes with a loud thud. Mom does not even stir.

Back in my room, I know I will not fall asleep, so I slip on a hoodie and grab my shoes, easing my window open high enough to slip out. I go to the side yard where we have a mini basketball court. It is the one thing my dad does not think I suck at, so to "encourage" me to practice, he had a nice hoop put in. But it really just means he expects me out there every day, all day. School does not matter, my messed-up dreams do not matter, nothing matters if I cannot sink every single free throw.

"You miss, you lose," he tells me.

I step back and take a shot from outside the arc, something he tells me not to try until the rest of my game is as good as his used to be. But Daddy's trashed right now and will not come out and critique me, so I take shot after shot until I finally make one.

There, Dad. Take that.

I spin the ball around and around in my hands, looking up at the glowing moon. My dreams will not haunt me tonight, and I am going to practice until I get this perfect. I bounce the ball, hard, once, twice, then line up the shot. I hear the swish the ball makes as it goes through the hoop. One. I take a breath, line it up and shoot. Swish. Two.

I shoot until the sun comes up.

18

- Addison -
Monday, December 12th, 2016

*F*riday night my parents took me to Zambini's for dinner to
celebrate my birthday. Aunt Carrie came too, and when we got home
she had made me a birthday cake. I wished for a normal night's sleep,
and for once, that wish came true. All weekend I dreamt mostly of
typical days at school, nothing new, nothing strange. So this morning, I
actually felt rested and ready for whatever the day brought.

"Addie!"

I turned at the sound of Cammie's voice. "Hey, Cam!" I
stretched out an arm, and she walked into me for a hug, almost
knocking me over in the process.

"Why do I feel like we haven't had a good chat in forever?"
she asked, linking arms with me and beginning to stroll down the halls
of Madison High.

"I know! How are you?" I stopped and turned to face her.

"I am fantastic! I got a new nail polish that hasn't chipped yet, and it's been like a week! So that's always a score. Oh! And Billy asked me out for this weekend," she said with a flip of her dark hair.

"Oh, really?" I asked, eyes wide. "That's great!"

"Yeah, but see, there's a catch." She starts walking again, avoiding eye contact.

"Cam..."

"You and Zach have to come with us. Like a double. It'll be so fun! I promise."

"Cam, I love ya, but you and Billy--"

"Addie, come on. Billy wants Zach there. We both get nervous, so it's just easier as a double date instead of just the two of us," she explained.

"Cam, I don't really see how you and Billy could be nervous around each other."

"What do you mean by that?" she asked.

"Well," I couldn't figure out how to phrase it so she would understand. "I mean, you and Billy are basically all over each other. You aren't even officially dating yet."

"We are not 'all over each other'." She turns back to look at me. "Are we?"

As if to answer this question, Billy comes strutting up (totally not nervous, in my opinion) and plants one on her.

"Hey, babe," he said.

"Yeah, you two are clearly not dating," I pointed out with a *really?* look to Cam.

She shrugged her shoulders and nuzzled closer to Billy. "Morning, babe," she said to him. I just laughed to myself and walked to class, leaving the two love-birds be.

In class, we were watching an informational video (that we wouldn't be tested on), so I took the opportunity to pull out Carrie's little journal and read more.

Dec. 20, 1997

I dream of Ben all the time now -- well when I'm not having my typical, insane dreams where someone is trying to kill me, hurt me, or torture me for information.

Those dreams have gotten worse -- as if that was humanly possible. The man in the hooded sweatshirt speaks now. His voice is raspy and terrifying. He seems to know everything about me, like he is in my mind all the time. So now, he is using my guilt against me. He will say "But what about Mitch?" or "How could you treat him this way? What has he ever done but love you?" It makes me want to throw up. I feel so bad.

But Ben is mysterious and intriguing, and we talk all the time now -- and kiss-- and other things.

I feel like I have to make it up to Mitch when I'm with him, even though he doesn't know what's going on. So I'll tell him I love him every few minutes or stay a little extra when we meet in the tree house. I let him go on and on about plans for our future together, meanwhile picturing the same future with Ben.

I suck, I know.

But Ben says he loves me. And my dreams aren't just little pictures in my mind like they are for the rest of the world. I know I'm different, and I know my dreams mean something. So wouldn't it mean something that I dreamt of Ben before I even talked to him in person, like fate was pushing me toward him all along?

I still love Mitch; I think I always will. But I think I'm in love with Ben, too. It's a different kind of love though. And he is different, not my usual type, and we are pretty much opposites in every way. But he says he loves me.

Oh, well, we'll see how it goes.

-Carrie

12/21/97

I stayed the night at Ben's last night and forgot I told Mitch I would meet him in the tree house· When he asked, I said I had stayed over at our friend Sandy's house and forgot to tell him·

-C

12/22/97

Ben says cool girls smoke· Since he is eighteen, he said he could buy me a pack· So I let him· It was awful; I thought I'd be sick· But he said I looked hot smoking· So I had him pick me up another pack· He's bringing it tomorrow when he picks me up to take me to "school"·

-C

What the heck is happening to Aunt Carrie? I wondered. She's a completely different person than in the beginning of this journal. She's extremely different than she is now -- like on another planet, different. There's no way this is her. I just can't believe she would do all of this and change so much because of this Ben guy.

19

"*H*iya, sweet pea! How was school?" Aunt Carrie asked while putting some dishes into the dishwasher.

"It was okay. Kinda boring," I answered, eyeing this woman who seems like a completely different person than the girl I'm reading about in the journals.

"Do you feel all caught up now?"

"Uh, for the most part."

"How's therapy going?"

Can people ask that question? Is that a common small talk conversation starter? Maybe in my family it is.

"Honestly, I hate it," I told her.

"Oh, I always hated that, too. But, you know, you oughta give meditation and yoga a try. It helps a million times more than some stuffy therapist. In my opinion, at least."

"Try telling my family that," I said. "I'm surprised they don't make me go more often."

"Oh, Hon. They're just worried about ya." She walked over from the sink so she was standing across from me at the island. "Do you want some cocoa?"

"Yeah, sure. That would be great!"

She went over to the cupboard and began making the cocoa. I just stood there watching, trying to think of the right questions to ask, what answers I needed, what I thought she'd actually tell me.

"Aunt Carrie?"

"Yes, sweetheart?"

"Would you mind if I asked you some questions?"

"Is this an interrogation or something? You know you can ask me anything. You don't need to be so formal." She handed me a mug of cocoa, and we both sat down at the table. "Here. You're out of marshmallows, so I put some whipped cream instead."

"Thanks," I told her, blowing on the top so I wouldn't burn myself.

"So, what questions do you have for your old aunt?" she asked with a loud slurp of her cocoa.

I needed to phrase the questions right so I wouldn't give her any suspicions about the journals.

"What was Madison High like when you and Mom went there?" I asked.

"Probably pretty much the same, just less technology." She chuckled then. "But every high school has the jocks, the nerds, the popular girls, and all that. Back in my day, basketball was the big thing. You either played it, or you dated one of the guys on the team. Or you wished you did."

"Did you?"

"Did I what?" She looked at me from over the brim of her mug.

"Did you date someone on the basketball team?" I questioned, even though I knew the answer to that one. I continued, "You said you had a high school sweetheart. Did he play?"

"Oh, right. Yes, he did. He was team captain."

"And you were cheerleading captain, right?"

"Yes ma'am. I can't remember anything from my cheerleading days anymore though."

"What was his name?"

"Whose name?" She looked almost startled that I had asked.

"The guy you dated."

She took the longest sip of hot cocoa I think anyone has ever taken in their life, obviously trying to buy some time. Just then -- as if by magic -- the doorbell rang. Aunt Carrie was saved by the bell.

"You want to get that?" she asked, standing up to put her mug in the sink.

"Sure," I told her, but sat there for a minute watching her. *Why is my own aunt such a mystery to me? Why won't she talk about high school or admit that she dated Mitch?*

I stood and walked over to the door, swinging it open.

"Lily?" I asked and stepped aside so she could come in. It was so odd seeing her there. She hadn't really talked to me at all the past few weeks. She hasn't responded to my texts and always had to "rush to class" when I saw her at school.

"Hi, Addison!" she sang, her voice much higher than usual.

"Hey, what's up?"

"Well, you weren't answering your phone, and neither was Cam, and your house is closer, so I just drove over here."

Why was she acting like this? Something must be wrong.

But before I could even ask what happened, she blurted out, "Brad asked me out!"

"Really? What did you say?" I tried to get her to come inside but she stood, frozen in place, on my front porch.

"Well, I didn't know what to say. I get so nervous when he is anywhere near me, so when he talks to me, it's like I can't even breathe."

"Okay?" I asked, not following.

"So he took my silence as a yes. He'll be at my house in a few hours, and I have no clue what to wear!"

She stepped to the side, and I just then noticed the huge duffel bag behind her, clothing spraying out of it.

"Lily, did you bring your whole closet?" I laughed.

"Pretty much." She tucked a piece of her fiery hair out of the way. "Please help me."

"Of course, come in!" I ushered her upstairs to my room.

"So where are you two going?"

"I don't remember. I forget if he said food or zoo. So it could really be anything. " She sat on the edge of my bed and buried her face in her hands.

I walked over and sat right next to her. "Lily?" I asked, brushing her hair out of her face as she wiped away a tear or two. "Do you want to be going out with Brad?"

"Yes. No. I don't know. I still really like him, but I can't handle getting my heart broken again." She looked ready to cry.

I took a breath. "It's hard, I know. But you should do what you want. If you aren't ready to go out with him, you don't have to. But if you want to give him a chance, it's only dinner-- or the zoo, apparently." That got a small laugh out of her.

"I guess you're right."

"Take it slow and see what he has to say. If all he says is crap, you never have to go out with him again. You've got the power here, it's your choice. Just speak up and tell him what you want."

She sat there for a minute, then stood and said, "I want to go."

"All right, then let's find you something to wear!"

An hour later we were in my room blasting music, and she sat at my desk while I curled her hair.

"I'm sorry," she said, and met my eyes in the mirror in front of her.

"Sorry for what?"

"For the way I've been acting; ignoring you and everything. I've been a sucky friend, and I'm sorry."

"Really, Lily, it's nothing." I looked away from the mirror, focusing on wrapping her hair around the curling iron.

"No, it's not nothing. One of my best friends was in a coma and then I treated her like dirt." She reached up and touched my hand with hers. "I'm really sorry, Addie."

"It's okay, Lily." I set down the curling iron and sprayed her hair in place.

"Oh! I love it!" she exclaimed. "I can never get it to curl like that."

"Now! You've gotta get back home before Brad comes to pick you up," I told her.

"Thank you for helping me! I don't know what I would've done without you." She gathered up her purse and bag full of clothes and headed for the door. But she turned around and said, "For the record, I was wrong. You haven't changed at all. You're still one of the nicest girls at Madison."

"Thanks, Lil," I said, looking away because I didn't know what else to say.

"And also," she added, "you and Zach are so perfect together! I hope things work out with Brad or I find my own 'Zach'."

"You will."

Then my phone buzzed: **New Text from Zach <3 Walker**

"Speak of the devil," I said with a smile.

"I've gotta go," Lily said, then smiled and added, "You go flirt with Zach."

20

- Addison -

Wednesday, December 14ᵗʰ, 2016

"**H**ey, beautiful!" Zach called, walking up to my front door that my mom had just decorated with a red and silver Christmas wreath.

"Hi," I said, a huge smile spreading across my face.

"Ready to go?" he asked, reaching across me to open the car door for me.

"Yes," I told him, stepping inside. "But... where exactly are we going?" I asked as he closed the door. I waited for him to walk around his car and get in. He turned the key in the ignition but remained silent. "Zach?"

"Yeah, Ad?"

"Where are we going?"

"That's top secret information."

"Zach, come on," I begged. "Where are we going?"

"It's a surprise. Just go with it," he ordered as he smirked at me, then backed out of my driveway.

We were talking about a project we have due for our history class when he turned down Pine Street.

I stopped in the middle of my sentence about the Anglo-Saxons and thought to myself, *The only reason I ever came down this road before was to go to-*

Jessica Clark's house.

"Zach? What are we doing here?" I questioned him.

"This is the surprise!" he said, putting the car in park and turning it off in The Clark's long driveway, right behind her mom's fancy car.

I stared up at the huge brick house with its wooden shutters and baby evergreen trees flanking the front porch. I knew this house well; I used to be here all the time as a kid.

I gulped. "It sure is a surprise," I said, turning in my seat to face him. "Zach, why are we here? I don't want to see your *cousin* right now."

"She just wants to help, Ad," he told me in a tone that made me feel like a five-year-old getting scolded.

"No, she really doesn't. Jess never does anything because she 'just wants to help.' I'm not going in there."

"Ad, come on. We need her help."

"With what, exactly?"

"Your training," he said simply.

Training? Finally! I thought. *I've been asking him for months to teach me the dreamer skills I need.*

"Well," I huffed. I really didn't want Jess' help. At all. But I *did* want to learn all the things she knew. "Fine. But I don't have to be nice to her if she isn't nice to me," I told him defiantly as I unbuckled my seat belt, got out of the car, and marched up her steps.

"Well, if it isn't the world's most precious dreamer-girl," Jess cooed when she opened the front door a moment later.

I stepped inside, already annoyed about this whole situation.

"Hey, cuz!" Jess exclaimed, wrapping Zach up in a hug. I rolled my eyes, and Zach eyed me -- a warning.

* * *

A half hour later we were all down in her basement. I was lying on the couch, Jess was sitting on the arm of the couch by my feet, and Zach was flipping through some book in the corner. *What is he reading? Do they seriously have textbooks on dreaming?* I wondered.

"You aren't trying hard enough," Jess complained.

"I am trying!"

"No, you aren't, or it wouldn't be taking so long!"

"It wouldn't be taking so long if you would just explain this all to me first!" I shot back.

"Come on, guys," Zach warned.

"I don't get why you can't just tell me what's going on and what you're doing before ordering me to dream something incredibly specific," I said, looking back and forth between the two of them.

They've been telling me to dream of myself in a field of purple wildflowers, with blues skies above me, as I'm wearing a striped sun hat and a breezy sundress. I am supposed to be alone in the field, except for a baby deer hiding along the tree line. I don't understand what all of that has to do with training though, or why it has to be so specific.

"We have to get a baseline," Zach explains. "We need to know how much you can do on your own."

"But why so specific?" I asked.

Jess chimed in, "Well, dreamer-girl, we know you can dream yourself to other places if you want to; Zach says you've done it before in dreams. We just want to see if you can dream to a place we tell you, that fits the details exactly."

"When Mitch trained us, he started with exercises like this," Zach added. "But, I have a feeling we can skip quite a few lessons with you."

"Why?" I asked.

"Because 'you're a natural', you're 'more talented than you know,'" Jess said, sarcasm and annoyance dripping from her twinkling voice.

"Just try one more time," Zach pleaded.

"Okay, fine," I said, settling in to the couch and getting comfortable.

Purple flowers. Sun hat. Field. Baby deer. Trees. Blue skies, I repeated over and over in my head, a mantra to fall asleep to, a dream to go to.

Then, suddenly, I was there. It was beautiful. Flowers everywhere, blowing gently in the wind. The sun streaming down, casting a golden glow everywhere.

"Well?" Jess' voice woke me from my dream. "What did you see?" she challenged.

I reached out and place my hand on her arm, thinking of that little dream again.

Jess sighed.

"What?" Zach asked, sounding worried, like maybe he thought she sighed because it didn't work and we'd have to start at square one.

"How did you do that so fast?" Jess questioned, staring jealous daggers.

I shrugged.

"Ha! Told ya she could do it," Zach told Jess, sounding proud. "My girl's a natural."

* * *

After two hours of them giving me a very specific place to go, dreaming into one of Jess' dreams, dreaming into one of Zach's dreams, or showing them dreams I had years ago, they finally decided it was time to take a break.

I had to admit, all this sleeping and dreaming had made me tired. *Funny, isn't it? How sleeping can make you want to sleep?*

"I can't find that one thing," Zach mumbled.

Jess must've known exactly what he was talking about – which annoyed me – because she got up and flipped to a specific page in the big, ancient-looking book Zach held. "Right here," she said.

He shook his head. "She can already do that, though."

"Do what?" I asked, but they talked on.

"I need more information," he said. "Where's that --"

"Green book?" she asked, and he nodded. "Upstairs in the den, third shelf, hidden behind the other books."

"Got it," he said and went upstairs to find this book.

"Look," Jess said, startling me with her intensity, as she walked over and sat next to me on the couch. "I need you to tell me what you know, how you can share your dreams. Who taught you that? Zach isn't here, and you may be fooling him, but you aren't fooling me, so just tell me the truth. Where did you learn all this stuff?"

"Jess, I don't know what you're talking about. I've never had anyone to help me and show me anything until today."

"Really, Addie?" she asked. It sounded weird hearing her call me that, after years of petty, stupid nicknames she gave me just to be mean. "I'm not buying it. We got through a whole training book in record time."

"Yeah, what's with those?" I asked. "Where did you get training books? Who even writes them?"

"I found some at an old used bookstore. The others Mitch gave me. Those are the better ones. Not sure where he got them from though. But, seriously, Addison. What's the deal with you? Why won't you just admit you know more than you're letting on?"

"Because I don't know more than I'm letting on."

"You've always done that," she said, turning away.

"Done what?" I asked.

"That whole 'I'm so innocent and naïve' act. You've always been Little Miss Perfect at everything without even trying. It's annoying."

"Jess, it isn't an act. I'm not pretending here. I know less about these twisted dreams than you do."

"Yet, you do everything perfectly? With no previous training? No clue what's going on?" she chuckled. "Figures, you'd be perfect at dreaming too."

"When did you know you were a dreamer?" I asked her.

"The eighth grade," she answered.

"Seriously?" I thought back, trying to remember just when our friendship fell apart. *Summer before eighth grade*, I reminded myself. "Is that why you --"

"Stopped talking to you? Don't flatter yourself, Addison. The world doesn't revolve around you. I stopped talking to everyone. I was scared to go to sleep – when I actually did get some sleep. I didn't have the energy to be '*The* Jessica Clark' always perfect and put-together, anymore. So, I stopped trying."

She stood and walked to the other side of the room. She played with a bunch of dried flowers in a vase on the mantle of the fireplace.

"Then," she continued. "I could just tell."

"Tell what?"

"That you were a dreamer too. I could see it in your eyes. But as always you were winning."

"Winning at what?" I asked Jess, standing and walking over to her. "This isn't a competition."

"Yes, it is. And you win. Every time. You were still doing amazing in school. You and Cammie became best friends, closer than we ever were. You looked beautiful, not like you hadn't slept in forever like I did. And that all really ticked me off."

"Jess," I said, suddenly realizing the reason behind her actions these last few years. "I am so sorry you felt that way. I never meant --"

"You didn't mean to do anything. That's the point, Addison. You never mean to. You don't mean to be perfect at dreaming when I suffered for years, not knowing what to do or how to make it better."

"I suffered for this too, Jess," I pointed out, my voice sounding small and weak.

"I doubt that."

How can she say that? Didn't she see me at school? I thought, shaking my head. I reached out, locking my hand around her wrist. She tried to pull away, knowing I would show her dreams.

"Addison, I really don't want to... I'm sorry," she said, actually sounding honest for once, as I let go of her hand. I could have shown her plenty more disturbing dreams than I did, but I just showed her two. "I guess I didn't make life any easier for you."

"No, you didn't," I admitted.

"I'm sorry, Addison. I guess I just figured if you had all this natural talent you, your dreams were probably of rainbows or you and Zach all 'happily ever after."

"Well, they aren't. Natural abilities don't do much for you if you don't know how to use them or what to do. You at least knew you were a dreamer and what that meant early on. I had no clue what was happening to me until I met Zach. This year. So while you thought my life was perfect, and were trying to get back at me for that, it really wasn't."

She stood there, staring at the carpet. "I don't really know what to say or how to fix this."

"We used to be best friends, Jess."

"I know we did. Do you think we could ever work our way back there? Maybe if I start trying to help you instead of breaking you down."

I thought for a minute. *It would be nice to have a friend who knows what's going on.*

"Sure, Jess. I don't know if we can ever be as close as we once were, but I'm willing to try to get to a good point with you."

She smiled, and that was the moment everything changed between me and Jessica Clark.

21

- Mitch -

Friday, December 16ᵗʰ, 2016

A whole week later and we still have no plan. Sandy
will not talk to me, only to Bill. That woman is
probably still mad at me even though it has been five
years.

I mean, sure, I called her up late one night,
slightly drunk. But she did not *have* to come over. She
did not *have* to get as drunk as I was. She did not
have to do anything. Just like *I* did not *have* to call
her the next day.

And sure, maybe I did not call her after that
night - or even speak to her for that matter - until
last year. "You only call when you need something,"
she says.

Sandy is not my girlfriend; she is barely even a
friend. But she is good at what she does, so I need
her on the dream team, not against us. And if that
takes some sweet talking from me, or having her
brother guilt her into it, so be it.

But let's just say we have had our fair number of
one-night-stands. The girl keeps running when I call,

so really it is her own fault. *Moth to the flame.* And sure, usually there are strings attached, like asking her for help with something within the dream realm. Or the latest, having her screw with Addison's mind during therapy sessions.

Since Sandy will not speak directly to me, I am forced to relay messages through her idiot of a brother. Bill is always screwing up some piece of the puzzle. Like this week, she said she would meet us somewhere to discuss Addison's progress in the "therapy" sessions.

Side note: Sandy's degree is real, that is for sure. Her pile of debt from student loans can attest to that. But her sessions with Addison are not quite as, shall we say, *confidential,* as they ought to be.

Anyway, Bill thinks Sandy said to meet at Blueberry Park, but what she really said was the park by Blueberry Street. Two very different places. When we do not show up, whose fault does Sandy say it is? Mitch. Now we have to wait until her highness can get away from work long enough to meet us a mere twenty minutes away from her house.

"Mitch?" Bill calls from the other room.

"What?"

"I can't get the Wifi to work."

"Figure it out," I bark and walk out the door.

I walk down the carpet meant to resemble grass all the way to the vending machine at the other end of the motel. I shove a twenty in the slot and then punch in the numbers for some microwaveable soup and a soda. A3, D7, and what the heck, C2 for a candy bar.

The soup can slowly crawls to the front the row, then clatters to the bottom of the machine. I reach under the rusting flap and grab it. Next comes the can of soda. But then, because it is just my luck, the machine makes a squealing sound and the candy bar suddenly stops coming forward. The coil keeps going around and around but does not push the candy bar any closer to the glass window.

"Come on!" I bang my fist on the glass.

"Is it the candy bars again?" a quiet voice comes from behind me.

I whip around and take in the sight of the teen girl standing there, arms crossed, a dollar bill between her fingers flitting in the wind. She is small and looks barely old enough to drive. She has reddish-brownish hair cut to about her shoulders just like Carrie had back in high school. Something about the girl's knowing grin reminds me of Carrie, too.

She takes a step forward and points behind me. "It's always the candy bars." Then she chuckles and sticks out her hand, "I'm Corrine."

I just look at her hand for a minute. *Did this girl's parents teach her nothing? She sees a thirty-something-year-old guy at a motel, of all places, and her first instinct is to introduce herself?*

I decide to play along. "Mitch," I tell her, shaking her hand.

"You new here?" she asks.

"About a month."

"A month? Wow, I'm surprised we haven't met yet! I know everyone here." Her eyes seemed to twinkle as she says this.

"Do you?" I ask with a smile. "How long have you been here?"

"Oh, I basically grew up here. Mom thought the motel business was for her, so we bought the place and fixed it up."

When she says this, I have to look around. *Fixed what up? This place is a dump,* I think.

"Yeah, so I've pretty much lived here my whole life. I work the front desk sometimes, well, when I'm not at school, that is." She looks at the vending machine. "May I?"

"Sure," I say, stepping aside.

She walks right up and rams her foot into the side of the machine. Two seconds later the candy flops down to the bottom. She reaches down, hands it to me, then slides her dollar in.

"How long will you be staying?" she asks.

"Not too sure yet--"

"Mitch!"

I turn and see Bill running down the hallway. "Mitch!"

"What's wrong now?" I ask angrily.

The girl takes her water bottle from the machine and shrinks back a bit, hiding in the shadows of the vending machine.

"It's Sandy. We've got to go."

"Oh, so now the princess decides she wants to help us?" I ask.

"She's in the hospital," Bill says in a daze.

"What?" There is a pinch in the pit of my stomach. *What is that feeling? Guilt? Fear?*

Bill just stands there, saying nothing.

"Bill, what happened?" I walk up and shake his shoulders. He just stands there. "Bill!"

The girl, Corrine, I think she said, looks at me and asks if we need to call someone. I tell her no, probably too harshly, and she runs off to the main office.

"Bill!"

"She overdosed."

"She what?"

He just stands there, unmoving, but slightly shaking. I run back to the room, grabbing his car keys off the table by the bed, and run back to where he stands. The whole while I have flashbacks of all the times I had to drive Bill to go help Sandy with something all throughout high school. Like when she crashed the car (not once but three times), or when she had to get her stomach pumped after a wild basketball party. I feel like Bill and I were always trying to save Sandy from herself.

And how ironic, a psychiatrist overdosing on prescription pills.

I find Bill still standing in the exact same place muttering over and over again, "I can't lose her. I promised Mom I'd keep her safe."

"I know, Bill, I know," I tell him, ushering him to the car, and knowing exactly how he feels. I had promised my own mom I would keep Meg safe.

RODGERS

> But I couldn't. No one could.

22

- Addison -
Friday, December 16th, 2016

*T*oday it snowed all day, big, white snowflakes coating the ground and everything in view. It was so exciting. I love it when it snows. There's just this sense of magic in the air when it snows. I feel like anything can happen, any wish can come true. But the snow can be cold, and right then, standing outside of the school waiting for Cammie to get done with her student council meeting, all I could think of was how cold I was and wishing I could get warm.

I looked up and saw Zach walking out of the school with a group of guys. He saw me and walked over.

"Hey, you," he said, pulling me in for a hug.

"Hey, yourself." See? Wishes do come true when it snows. I wished to be warm, and I definitely was in his arms. "You know, you just made my wish come true," I said and turned my face up to look at him.

"I know," he shrugged. "I am the guy of your dreams after all." He had that cute, crooked grin on his face.

"You're going to use that line a lot, aren't you?" I asked hugging him tighter.

"Oh, yeah." He laughed and kissed the top of my head. "I'm your dream guy. You know it. I heard some freshman girls called me a dreamboat." He chuckled, "Little do they know, right?"

I playfully hit his arm. "Oh, don't go getting a big head."

"Too late. Anyway, I got the girl of my dreams, so it all worked out. So...what are you doing out here? It's freezing."

"Waiting for Cam. We are going for coffee to 'strategize' for tonight."

"Strategize? I thought we were just all going to dinner. What's the big deal?"

"You know Cam," I said, just as the door creaked open and she slipped out.

"I know, I know, the meeting ran late. I'm sorry!" she called to me, pulling on her gloves with the pearls on them that she said were not very warm, but she still wore them everyday. "And what were you saying about me?"

"That you are my bestest friend in the whole wide world."

"Oh! Well then, keep talking," she said, batting her lashes.

"I've gotta get going," Zach announced.

Cam dramatically threw her arms up in front of her eyes.

"What are you doing?" I asked her.

"I'm covering my eyes, so you can say goodbye."

I laughed, Zach shrugged, and Cammie told us both to hurry up.

"See ya later," he told me.

"Bye, Zach." I put my hand behind his neck and pulled him down for a kiss.

"Bye, Zach!" Cam called, still covering her eyes.

Once Zach had walked away, Cam shivered and said, "You know what we need? Coffee!"

* * *

We went to the local burger place because Zach hadn't been there yet. He really liked it there and claimed the fries were as good as Sal's, which is like blasphemy in Madison. Other than that, Billy and Zach got along really well and were watching some game on the flatscreen and talking like old friends. Cammie kept saying, "Isn't this perfect! We are like the perfect group, aren't we?"

Later that night after dinner, the four of us decided to take a walk to the town square. There's a gazebo and some park benches, nothing too special, but this time of year they usually string up lights, and it looks really pretty.

"Hey, Ad! Look! It's snowing!" Cammie squealed, sidling up to me and squeezing the sleeve of my puffy winter coat. "I LOVE SNOW!" She let go of me and twirled in circles in the middle of the street.

"Hey, beautiful," Billy said to her, taking her hand.

"Isn't this perfect?" she asked for the thousandth time tonight. "Don't you just love snow?" she said turning to Billy.

"Love it!" he said so enthusiastically you could tell he would agree with her on anything if she kept smiling like that.

"It's incredible, isn't it?"

"Incredible," Billy agreed.

Snow began falling faster and heavier. Big white flakes landed on us and swirled all around us. It looked like a scene from a snow globe.

I shivered as a freezing wind blew by, snowflakes carried by it. I turned to my side and saw that Zach was right next to me now. He smiled and took my hand in his. I instantly felt warmer. I looked up a little bit ahead of us and saw that Cammie and Billy were still holding hands. He smiled and twirled her around and around. They looked so happy. Then they stopped walking and started kissing. Something about this felt familiar, like a distant memory or dream.

I looked up at Zach, who laughed and said, "They might be a while."

We strolled hand in hand past a few buildings, coming up to the main square. We passed a coffee shop that just opened a few weeks ago. They had live music playing inside.

Zach turned to look at me. "Have you ever danced in the snow?" he asks grinning.

I couldn't say that I had. He pulled me closer, and we danced right there in the middle of the street, music floating out into the air from inside.

I realized then why tonight felt so familiar. This happened in one of my dreams back when I was asleep. I could tell he remembered that dream, too.

I tipped my head up so I could look Zach in the eye, a big smile spreading across my face. "It's happening. The dream is coming true."

"Yes, it is."

We were like that for a few minutes, maybe longer, swaying gently back and forth as the snow fell down around us, grinning like idiots. It was like our little secret from our own little world; a story from somewhere only the two of us knew. We also are the only two people who know about the dream that came right before, both of us wondering if that vision would come true, too. In that dream we were engaged, starting a life together. I sometimes wondered if that would happen, if we would make it when we had so much against us, when we had people like Mitch against us. But then moments like tonight happen, a dream come true - literally - and I knew that we would make it.

Flecks of snow fell on his dark hair. I reached up, running my hands through his hair, trying to catch the snowflakes. Then I felt his one hand cupping my face and his other tangle up in my hair, too. He brought his lips down to mine, and I felt his warm breath as I closed my eyes. As he kissed me there in front of the twinkling lights of the town gazebo, snow falling down, I couldn't help but agree with Cammie and think, *Isn't this perfect? Isn't this incredible?*

Yes, Addison, it is, I told myself. *Perfect moments do exist. Dreams do come true, not just the bad ones, but the good ones, too.*

I wondered if this is what love feels like, because if it is, I really love falling in love. I told myself to stop thinking so much and just enjoy the moment. I felt him pull me closer, and I smiled while he kissed me, happy to have this little piece of forever, a moment frozen in time in our own little snow globe.

23

- Mitch -

Friday, December 16th, 2016

The smell is what hits me first. Hospitals have a way
of smelling...sickly clean. There is an ever-present
scent like bleach, sterile and fluorescent bleach,
like you can smell the white-ness of the hospital.
Have you ever noticed how bright a hospital is? I do
not mean bright as in cheery, happy bright -- because
it most certainly is not that. I mean bright as in
blinding, white, crisp. White walls; white sheets;
pale, white faces; and stark lighting flickering
overhead.

      Hospitals make me feel sick. They remind me of
all the nights I wound up here growing up with Meg,
Mom, and even Dad. Those nights were awful. Doctors
and nurses asking questions I could not simply answer.
Meg screaming or crying like a toddler -- I hated it
when she cried.

"Bill Hardy," Bill tells the receptionist, bringing my mind back to the present. "I'm looking for Sandy. She's my sister," he informs her.

She checks a clipboard. "Room 203," the nurse says pointing to the left.

"203, 203," Bill repeats until at last we reach the room.

I look in the room and have to stop just outside, on the threshold. Bill does not even notice that I do not come in. I stand there like a ghost, watching him running up to Sandy's side.

It was not too long ago that I rushed in like that to see Meg. That time was the worst. I did not think she would make it. There was a point during her senior year when she started having seizures because of the dreams. I could not do anything and did not know how to help her. The seizures calmed down for a while until shortly after Zach was born, then they came back.

"Sandy!" Bill was crying over her lifeless body that was basically being kept alive by the machines attached to her. "Don't die. You can't leave me."

Those two were always close. Sometimes I wonder if it was the dreams that kept them close. He was always protecting her.

But I could not protect Meg. She was too far gone by the time I could control any part of the dream realm.

I listened to the steady heart monitor beep, beep, beep, beep, beep.

How many pills did she take? I wonder. *What pills did she take?*

Beep, beep, beep, beep.

A team of doctors rushes behind me carting a person on a gurney and shouting codes and orders.

I look up, take a breath, and stare into the bright light above me.

Sandy's gone…

24

- Addison -
Friday, December 16th, 2016

*L*ater that night I sat in my room flipping through Carrie's journals and rereading some of the pages. *I need more answers than this,* I thought. *This isn't enough. What did she do to get rid of her dreams?*

There was a knock on my bedroom door.

"Come in," I called out.

"Hey, sweetie," my mom said, the door open just a crack.

"Hey, Mom. What's up?"

"Can we talk?"

"Of course."

I shoved the journal into my opened backpack and slid over to make room for her. She climbed onto my bed and wrapped her arm around me.

"How's school been?"

"Good. I finally feel caught up," I offered.

"That's great! I told you it wouldn't take long at all."

I pulled a blanket up over our feet.

"So," she started.

"So."

"How are things with Zach?" she asked. I could see the conflict on her face; she loved to chat about boys and all that stuff and was excited that "Addie's got a boyfriend!" But at the same time, her little girl was clearly growing up.

"Things with Zach are great," I told her.

"You seem happy."

"I am," I admitted. I could see the tears forming in her eyes. Her child, who had so much happen in the past year, was happy.

She choked back the tears. "I'm glad, honey."

"Thanks, Mom."

"And you know that you can talk to me about anything, right?"

"I know, Mom," I told her with a smile.

She looked around my room, then something seemed to click in her mind. She turned to me, "Oh! I almost forgot why I came in here."

I waited for her to continue. She took a breath and said, "Honey, we just got a call from Dr. Hardy's office."

"What? Do they want to bring me in for some testing? Do they think I've lost my mind?" I asked, teasing.

Her mouth formed a tight line. "Addison, Dr. Hardy passed away tonight."

"What?"

It was such a shock. I just saw her a few days ago.

"They called because you have an appointment scheduled for tomorrow morning, and they didn't want us driving all the way out there. Her receptionist will be sending us a list of other specialists in the area shortly."

"What happened?" I asked, sitting up completely straight.

"They didn't say." She rubbed my back gently. "Are you okay, honey? I know this is a tricky situation. I know you were very comfortable with her. We will find you another doctor you trust soon, okay? But in the meantime, please talk to me. You can tell me anything."

I almost had to laugh at that thought. Comfortable around her? How could I be? Although, I guess I told her a lot about my dreams and everything. Which is odd, because I didn't plan on telling her any of it, but I always felt compelled to tell her.

I wonder what happened to her, I thought.
"Come talk to me whenever you want," my mom said.
"Don't worry, Mom. I will."
She kissed my forehead and left the room.

25

- Mitch -
Wednesday, December 17th, 1997

Carrie was not at school today. She did not answer my phone calls and did not meet me in the tree house like she was supposed to. Around ten o'clock, I leave the tree house and head home. If she has not come by now, she will not come.

I creep in the back door, quietly making my way upstairs. When I left, Mom was sound asleep, and I did not want to risk waking her if she was finally getting a good night's sleep.

Just as I reach the top step I hear someone yell, "Mitch!" Meg screams from down the hall.

I run into my parent's room. "Meg! What's wrong?"

"It's Mom," she says between shaky breaths. "I can't get her to wake up."

"Mom?" I ask, as if she will respond to me when she has not been responding to Meg. "Mom!"

Meg starts crying, hard.

"She'll be fine. Don't worry. She's okay," I say calmly while trying to shake my mother awake.

"No!" my mom screams. "No! I won't do it! I won't do it!"

"Mom, you're okay! Stop," I try to tell her.

She starts convulsing, and it is almost too terrifying to watch. She is writhing around on the floor, screaming bloody murder.

"Where's Dad?" I yell over her screams.

"He's still out," Meg says.

Out? I wonder. *Where is Dad at ten at night?*

"Do something!" Meg yells.

"I can't. She can't hear me. I don't know what to do," I admit.

"I can help her. I think," she says, but she does not sound so sure.

"What could you possibly do to help Mom right now, Meg?"

"I've been practicing this thing. Hang on." She reaches out, cupping Mom's face with her hands. She takes a breath, squeezes her eyes shut, and grips my mom's face a little tighter.

What the heck is she doing?

Meg screams and jumps back.

"The dreams are bad. They're too much for her," Meg says, breathing hard.

"Meg, how do you know that?" I yell, eyes wide.

"I saw what she was seeing."

"How?" I ask, but she ignores me and goes back over to Mom.

"It's all right, Mom, I'll take some of the dreams," she says in a childlike voice. She holds onto Mom again, screaming while doing whatever witchcraft she is doing. Then Meg starts shaking, too.

I look down at my two family members, writhing around in pain.

"Make it stop!" I yell out. To who? I have no clue. "Stop it!" I yell, slamming my fist on the floor.

I do not know what to do. I run over to the phone and dial Carrie's home number.

"Come on, answer! Carrie, I need you," I say quietly as the phone rings on and on.

Finally a click.

"Hello?"

"Carrie?!"

"No, this is Annie." A pause. "Mitch?"

"Is Carrie there? I need to talk to her."

"No, she's out. I thought she was with you?"

"She isn't." *Where is she?*

"Do you want me to give her a message?"

"No," I bark and hang up.

"Mom, please stop. Wake up," I beg.

After a few minutes, I swear it gets worse. I look down at the phone. What else is there to do? So with shaking fingers, I dial three numbers.

"What's your emergency?" she asks.

How do I even explain this? What can I say?

* * *

Hours later, Meg is stable and sitting in her hospital bed drinking orange juice. But they are still running tests on Mom.

Nurses keep asking me questions. Questions I cannot answer.

I left a note for Dad at home and called the house multiple times in case he came home, but he still is not here, so he must not have even come home yet.

"Mr. DeMize?" a doctor in a bright, white lab coat comes up behind me.

"Yes?"

"We've run all the tests we can. Not much is showing up as being abnormal. We aren't entirely sure yet what caused her episode tonight. We have, however, stabilized her. You can go see her soon."

"Thank you," I tell him, starting to walk to her room.

"Actually, there's more," he says, catching my arm before I could leave. "Could we sit for a minute?" he asks politely.

"Uh, sure."

"I'm not quite sure how to put this, but any information you can give us will help us better treat your mother."

"Okay?" I say.

"But, I'm wondering...how long has your mother been experiencing schizophrenic episodes?"

"Schizophrenia?" I ask. *She does not have schizophrenia! She has nightmares; horrible, horrible nightmares! We all do.* But I could not tell him that. He would not believe that is all this is.

"It's not as uncommon as you'd think. However, in her case, it is pretty severe. Has this been affecting her day-to-day life and ability to function or work?" he asks.

I think about it. "She doesn't work. She got fired a bit ago," I blurt out before I can stop myself.

"It'll be all right, son. I think having her stay overnight for observations would do her a world of good."

"What are you going to do to her?" I ask.

"She is in good hands, I assure you. This hospital has one of the best psychiatric wards associated with it in the region," he explains as if this helps.

"Psychiatric ward? You can't put her there," I say, standing abruptly.

"I'm not saying for sure that's what we are doing yet."

"You can't do that at all!" I yell. *Who is this guy to think my own mom needs to be put in a psych ward? She will be fine. She will get over it. I am going to figure these dreams out soon and help her, and me, and Meg. A psych ward will only make things worse. They cannot help her there!*

"No, no, you can't do that!"

"I'm sorry, Mr. DeMize. But we have to do what's best for her. Once your father gets back in town, I will discuss this further with him"

I do not know where my dad is and why he is not here helping us, so when they asked, I said he was away on business.

"I'll be in touch when we know more. You should probably go get some sleep," the doctor says with a kind smile.

How am I supposed to sleep when they are considering locking my mother away somewhere?

* * *

A few days later, I sit at the kitchen table with Meg, drinking coffee because I have been sleeping even less than usual lately.

My dad comes strolling in.

"How's Mom?" Meg asks, over-enthusiastically considering the options we have.

"She'll be fine. They're moving her to The Haven as we speak."

"The Haven?" I yell, standing up and stepping in front of my father's face.

The Haven is the psychiatric ward they have been talking about placing my mother in. "The best in the region," they say. "She'll be out of there in no time," my dad tells Meg.

But no one ever leaves The Haven. They send the worst cases there. It is not a week's stay sort of place. No. This place is forever.

Meg starts to cry. "They'll kill her!" she yells again and again and again.

My father slams his beer bottle on the counter, startling both me and my sister. "Enough, already. It's better this way. I've been saying she needs help for years."

"You're wrong, Daddy. You're wrong!" Meg cries.

"You'll be next," he says and takes a swig of his drink.

You'll be next? What kind of a--

I do not even finish the thought before my fist is flying directly into his face.

In an instant he has me up against the wall. His face is too close to mine, smells too much of alcohol when it is only two in the afternoon. "You will show me some respect!" he yells in my face.

ECHO

"She's your daughter!" I yell back. *What a sad excuse for a father,* I think. *Telling your daughter you'll lock her up next.*

"She's insane!" he says to me, but of course she hears and the crying gets worse, sounding almost animal-like. "Look at her!" he says, pushing me further against the wall. "It's only a matter of time, Mitchell. You might even wind up there, too."

He lets go finally. I rub my throbbing throat.

I walk over to Meg and try to help her up.

"I won't go there," she tells me through her tears.

"You won't," I tell her. I look up and glare at my father.

"I need more beer," he announces.

"No, you really don't."

"Mitchell!" he yells, closing the refrigerator door. Hard.

"Come on, Meg." I grab her arm and pull her out the back door with me.

"Where are we going?" she asks.

"Far away from him until he sobers up," I say.

"Please don't take me there," she says, and it takes me a minute to realize she means The Haven.

"I will never take you to The Haven," I tell her. "Because there's nothing wrong with you."

Little do I know that was the first promise to my sister I would break. The second is promising to always protect her son.

26

- Addison -

Saturday, December 17th, 2016

"**H**ey, kiddo! Guess what! I'm staying through New Year's!"
Aunt Carrie squealed running into the kitchen and squeezing my
shoulders.

"That's awesome!" I told her as she hugged me from behind.
More time to get some answers out of you, I thought.

"I'm running to the store for your mama real quick. Need
anything?" she asked.

"Actually, I still have to pick something up for Mom for
Christmas."

"Why don't you come with me? It'll be fun!"

"Okay!" I grabbed my purse off the island, and the two of us
were out the front door.

"So, where to first?" she asked, pulling out of the driveway. "I'm
sure the stores are different from the last time I was here."

I almost had to laugh at that thought. "Aunt Carrie, this is
Madison Town. Nothing ever changes here. I'm sure the stores are

the same as when you were my age."

"Very true!" she agreed. After a minute sitting at a stoplight, she clapped her hands together. "Oh! Let's go to that cute little boutique off Seventh!"

"Oh, yeah! That place is so cute!" So we drove through town, past the town center, and down Seventh, where they were hanging wreaths with bows on every lamp post.

"Oh, I forgot how much I love it here at Christmas!" she said.

We pulled up in front of a shop with a striped awning and a sign that read: Jennie's Treasure Cove. The shop had been there for as long as I could remember. I had only met the infamous Jennie once. Now she's in a nursing home, and her granddaughter runs the store. Since the granddaughter took over, they've gotten some new stuff, like jewelry some local ten-year-old makes and paintings a kid in my English class paints.

We walked in the door and a bell jingled above us. "Hey there!" Jennie's granddaughter called from behind the register.

"Hi, Lexie!" I replied.

"We just got some new beach-themed things in the back corner over there!"

"Mom loves the beach!" I said turning to Aunt Carrie.

"She does! Let's go check it out," she agreed.

There was a table full of aqua-colored Christmas ornaments and beaded flip-flops. I was looking through the sea-glass key-chains when Carrie said, "So, what did you get that boy of yours for Christmas?"

I smiled at the key-chains. "Nothing yet. I don't know what to get."

"Oh, I can help with that!"

I'm sure you can, I thought.

"Tell me about him," she ordered, picking up a pack of napkins with shells that said "Seas the day!"

"What do you want to know?"

"Well, I've met him, so I know what he looks like -- nice pick by the way!" I blushed at her comment. "So tell me about his personality or," she looked around and then pulled me over to a table of guys' stuff and said, "how you feel around him."

"Happy," I told her without even thinking about it.

She smiled. "That's good. That's really good, sweetie...okay, tell me more."

"Safe," I added.

"Safe. That's even better," she said with a knowing smile. *When you dream like we do, feeling safe is all you can ask for.*

We looked at decks of cards, socks, little games for work desks, and calendars. But nothing seemed like Zach.

"What's your favorite thing about him?" She picked up a tie. "Looks-wise, I mean."

"His eyes," I answered and practically zoned out thinking about his blue eyes.

"Oh, you're an eyes girl? Interesting." After a minute she squealed, "Oh! This is perfect!"

I was back looking at the beach section. I had found some ornaments and a frame made out of shells for my mom. I turned around, "What?" I asked.

"Would you say that when you're with him," a big grin spread across her face, "time stands still?" She whipped her hands around from behind her back and was holding up a watch.

I laughed at her pun, "Aunt Carrie, that's perfect!"

It was a really nice dark brown watch, classy; he'd love it! I was getting money from my purse to buy the watch and the stuff for my mom when my aunt got a funny look on her face.

Then she put her hand on my arm and said, "I'm so happy for you, Addie. Don't let this one get away, okay?"

I could tell in her eyes she was thinking about her own boy that got away, or rather, the one she let go for someone else. The boy that, after she let him go, became a completely different person. *I wonder if she ever wonders about what a life with him would be like?*

"Don't worry, I won't," I told her, and I really meant it.

Then she proceeded to try on every ridiculous hat in the store while I just laughed along. Leave it to Aunt Carrie to find the crazy hats! The longer we were there I got the feeling she genuinely loved this one bright teal sun hat with a yellow bow on it. I had handed it to her as a joke, but she hadn't put that hat back yet and tried it on three times.

"Hey, Addie, grab that matching one over there! We can be twinsies!" she called over to me pointing to a yellow sun hat with a teal bow.

Nope. She's definitely not kidding now.

* * *

Later that night I sat up in my bed unable to sleep, and I read more of Carrie's journal. These were the last few pages in the book with the blue bow. I planned on bringing this one to Zach tomorrow to read, and then I was going to start the next one. I turned the page.

12/23/97

    Ben and I skipped school today· He took me to a buddy of his' place· They were drinking and doing drugs· Mitch would never take me to a place like that; he's too good· But Ben said it would be rude if we left· Then I just felt so calm, which is really nice compared to the guilt and dream-related-terror I've been experiencing otherwise· So I stayed a while·

    When I got home, Annie was furious· She covered for me with mom and dad, but she was livid· I used some words with her I never used to say· Then, because I was mad, I stole her favorite eyeliner from her drawer·

    I don't usually wear makeup, but Ben likes it, so I'm going to start· And it'll really tick off my sister, so why not?
    -C

12/24/97

    Mitch freaked when he saw all the makeup on me today· "It's too dark; I've never seen you like that," he said· I told him he doesn't own me and walked away·

    I got my bellybutton pierced· All the pop stars have it like that· And I bought more eye makeup too·
    -C

What is happening to her? I wondered.

I felt my eyelids begin to droop. I was so tired, but I flipped to the next page, the very last one in this book. It was a very short entry, from the end of December. I guessed each journal was about a month of her life. I mustered up the energy to at least stay awake to read the last page.

The last entry in the blue journal read:

12/31/97

    Tonight was the annual New Year's Eve party at one of our neighbor's houses· Practically the whole town is invited· I snuck off to find Ben for midnight·

Then Mitch found the two of us···

I never in my life thought I would ever say the words I did as I closed my aunt's journals. But I did. I actually, honestly, looked at the ground and said ever-so-quietly, "Poor Mitch."

27

- Addison -
Wednesday, December 31ˢᵗ, 1997

I open my eyes and look all around. *Where am I?* I wonder.

Everything is fuzzy, like the whole earth got blanketed with a dense fog.

I feel...off. Not myself. Almost like I'm floating. I realize I must be dreaming. This all seems too strange.

"Carrie!"

Carrie?

I see a teenage guy walking toward me. His smile is intense, swoon-worthy, reaching all the way to his dark brown eyes.

"Hey, baby," the words come out of my mouth. But they don't sound like me. It sounds like Aunt Carrie. But I *know* I'm the one who just spoke.

"Come with me," he says, tugging on my hand, pulling me further into the grey haze.

I follow him.

Why am I following him? I tell my legs not to move, *don't you dare follow.* But I don't seem to have control over myself.

"Carrie," he says with a sigh, pulling me close.

I'm not Carrie! I want to scream. But what really comes out is, "I love you, Ben."

Ben?!

"I love you, too, Carrie."

The guy -- the Ben from the journals, I'm guessing -- runs a hand through his sandy-colored hair, eyeing me. Then he leans down and starts kissing my neck.

Get off! I try to shout. I try to push him off, but he won't stop.

"I love you, Ben," I involuntarily say again.

I hear chanting in the background, floating over loud music. "Ten! Nine! Eight!"

"We should get back," he says in a way that is really saying "I never want to leave here."

"Yeah, we should," is what comes out of my mouth next, but then I just tip my head back and his lips are on mine. *What is happening?* I am freaking out now. I try to pull away, but it's like my body won't listen to my head. It's almost like I'm just watching this happen.

"Five! Four!" the chanting continues.

"Run away with me," he mumbles.

"Anywhere," I agree while my mind is yelling at my aunt.

"Three! Two!"

What's with the chanting?"

"One! Happy New Year!" the crowd yells out down the hall.

"Happy New Year, babe," the body I'm trapped in tells Ben.

"Carrie?" a voice weighed down by hurt and anger cuts through the darkness as a light does, too.

The sudden light is too bright. After a second I realize I, as Carrie, am in a closet. The guy I'm guessing is Ben is wrapped around me. Both of us are looking at the doorway where a boy stands, dark hair falling down in front of his one eye. But the other eye is a sparkling blue, like Zach's but not quite as bright.

"Carrie?" the boy asks again.

"Mitch, it's not what it--"

"I got this," Ben says to me, cutting me off. "Listen," he starts, standing up and towering over the other boy.

"Ben--" my voice starts.

Ben starts talking in a very unapologetic voice, "I'm sorry you had to find out this way, Mitch. Really."

That's Mitch?

"Carrie?" the boy - Mitch - asks again as if he can't believe Carrie is the one standing in front of him.

"Please let this be a dream," I say under my breath.

"Carrie?" Mitch asks yet again.

"Hey, man, it's not your fault. You just weren't what she needed," Ben says.

He takes a breath to continue, and in a flash I'm up and pushing him back. "You're only making it worse, Ben," I tell him.

"Carrie?"

"Mitch, I am so sorry." Tears are rolling down my face. "I never wanted to hurt you."

"Too late," he says and walks away.

Run after him! I yell, but the words never leave my mind, and my feet never leave the ground. *Carrie run! Go find Mitch. If you can fix things with him maybe things would be different. Don't be the thing that breaks him,* I beg.

How can the boy I just saw be the same guy who taunts me while I sleep?

This has to be a dream.

28

- Addison -
Saturday, December 17ᵗʰ, 2016

I sat up in bed, breathing hard. *What just happened?* I put a hand over my heart attempting to calm the craziness inside. My other hand brushed against something, paper, slicing my finger ever-so-slightly. *Stupid papercut,* I thought, and brought my finger up to my mouth. I grabbed the booklet of papers that had just cut me and looked at them.

It was Aunt Carrie's journal, opened up to the very last page.

12/31/97

Tonight was the annual New Year's Eve party at one of our neighbor's houses. Practically the whole town is invited. I snuck off to find Ben for midnight. Then Mitch found the two of us...

Did I just dream about that journal entry? The thought was just too crazy. There was no way I could have had a dream about that situation after reading four sentences about it. Right?

I stood up and began to pace the length of my room. My room felt too tight, too dark all of a sudden. I practically ran over to the wall and flipped the switch. Light flooded into my room as I tried to catch my breath.

It was all just too weird. I'd never had a dream as if I was someone else before. I didn't even think that would be possible. But that dream was most definitely not about me. There's no way.

It all lines up with Carrie's journal.

That's it! I realized. *Everyone knows you dream about what you fall asleep thinking about. So obviously, I fell asleep right after reading that journal. The thought of it probably just worked its way into my dream.*

Unless...

I thought back over all the dreams while I was in the coma. *Were any of them a dream where I was in someone else's body?* I wondered.

I thought about them all: when Zach came over in the Pizza Palace uniform, when the rock broke apart, when I first met Zach, when Jess tried to steal him away, when I found Zach and saved him.

Wait a second...

In that part of the dream I thought about him and where he could be. I remembered my mind running through all the memories I had with him from the short time I had known him. It was like watching a montage in a movie. But then the dream changed, and I saw Zach hurt and alone, and suddenly I was there with him.

It was like I dreamed myself there.

What did you just do, Addison? I asked myself. *There's no way. Right? I couldn't possibly have just dreamed myself into one of my aunt's dreams. Or did I?*

Again, I wondered, *What did you just do, Addison?*

29
- Mitch -
Monday, December 19th, 2016

The funeral is today. I do not go. I know that I
should. Bill is really the only friend I've got. But I
cannot make myself go there.

I hate funerals. Although, who really likes them?
They remind me of the day we buried my mother.
She had been at The Haven for about a year before
things got bad. She stopped taking the medicine there;
I guess she hid the pills in her pillow. Visiting
rights were taken away one day. Apparently Mom had a
fit in the common room and caused all the other
patients to throw a fit as well.

Meg cried really hard that night. "They'll kill
her," I remember her saying to me. "They'll kill her,
and I can't even see her now."

Later that night she tried to dream with my mom.
She explained later that they had a telepathy thing
going. Most nights they dreamt the same things. I
never knew that. I hoped maybe I dreamt the same as
them. We are all related after all.

But Meg explained some of their dreams to me, and I had never had a dream like that before. Here, I thought my dreams were bad. Their dreams were on a whole other level. They were almost at Addison-level. I am surprised she has not gone to the nut house yet. I guess it is only a matter of time.

It was only a few weeks after they stopped letting us visit her that the phone rang.

"Hello, this is Grace from The Haven. Is your father home?"

I remember that phone call clear as day.

Of course, as always, my father was not home. He was probably at a bar or at work.

Three days later I stood in the pouring rain and threw dirt over my mother's grave. Meg stood next to me; she seemed to be the only one holding it together, which was surprising. I think she was just numb that whole week.

My dad was blubbering like a baby, and that really ticked me off. He did not love her. Maybe he did before, but certainly not now. He was never home, and when he was, he was drunk. She deserved so much more than him. She deserved a man who could protect her from her dreams, not one who was a living nightmare.

The worst part was seeing Meg look down at the flowers in her hand and whisper, "Dad's right. I'm next."

She was shaking uncontrollably. Her breathing did not sound normal at all. "I'm next," she said again and again and wrapped her arms around her stomach like she was trying to physically hold herself together.

"Mitch, I'm next," she said, falling into my arms, sobbing and panicking, as if the angel of death was running toward her right that second.

The look in her eyes was the saddest and scariest thing I have ever seen.

So instead of going to Sandy's funeral, I stayed in Bill's apartment for the day. The shows on TV are crap these days. When I was in high school, they were so much better. Everything now is just drama and "they lived happily ever after."

Happily ever after is a lie. It doesn't happen, trust me.

What you really get in this thing called life is the opposite of happily ever after. You get starting your junior year on top of the world with the greatest - and hottest - girl at school, and you end the second quarter standing in front of a closet watching your girl all over some other guy. So much for happily ever after.

I am convinced true love does not exist. I am thirty-six years old. I know things. And one of those things I know is that no one is ever happy. There is a lot that goes on behind closed doors that the rest of the world will never know about.

People used to look at Carrie and me and say how perfect we were. They did not know about the nightmares.

From the outside looking in, I had the perfect family, but no one heard my sister's screams, saw my mother having panic attacks, or knew that my father, Mr. Nice-Guy, was all an act.

The whole town thought Sandy had her life together. I mean, for Pete's sake, her job description was helping other losers get their life together. No one saw her prescribing and popping pills every night.

People think Addison is Madison High's perfect little sweetheart. They do not know what lies in her future.

It is a pattern, this life.

Being a dreamer, you only have two options: change completely, like Carrie, or go completely crazy, like my mother and my sister and a whole line of DeMizes before them.

Precious little Addison is on the road to crazy town. It is only a matter of time. And quite honestly, it is better that way. She is too strong. It is for her own good, really. I have to give her a little nudge in the direction Meg took. She cannot get rid of her powers like Carrie did. It would be a waste. But if I make her think she's crazy, she will have no choice but to turn to me for help. Then I will "help" her and get her fully on my side.

I cannot have someone with her capabilities against me. I cannot. Once I get her to trust me, I can manipulate the boy as well.

* * *

Hours later and Bill still is not back.

I am in his "kitchen," opening and closing door after door. There is no food in this place. Nothing. Finally, I find it. A cardboard box shoved behind the stove I doubt has ever been used. It is a case of beer, only one missing.

I grab one out of the box and blow the dust off the top. I listen as the can opens -- what a great sound. I gulp down most of it right then. I grab two more and go back to the other room. I get comfortable in the recliner he has. *Only decent thing in this place.*

Another hour and a few beers later I figure it is about time I get to work on driving the girl crazy, don't ya think? I close my eyes and search my mind. I picture her lying in that hospital bed dreaming her crazy dream.

Then, just like that, I have found her. It is the middle of the afternoon, but it appears she's taking a nap.

Perfect.

It is less than ten seconds before I am in her head, in her dream. She is dreaming about Zach again. *Figures.*

I make sure Zach is not actually dreaming this dream, too, and he is not, which will make it easier for me. It is less draining to just work my magic on one mind instead of two. She already looks on edge, and she does not even know I am in her dream yet. *This is going to be too easy.*

"Hello, Addison," I say. Her head snaps in my direction.

I dream I am on the other side of her now. "Hello, again," I say. She is startled. *Good.*

Then I dream myself right up behind her so she can just feel me breathing down her neck, too close for comfort.

"What are you doing here?" she asks, fear weighing down her voice.

"You know what I'm doing here," I point out. I do not move, I stay right there behind her. She does not move either. I watch her shoulders rise and fall heavily. She is nervous.

"What did Carrie do?" I ask harshly.

"I don't know yet."

"Addison," I start, but she turns around, levels her eyes with mine.

"Don't you think if I knew, I would've done the same thing just to get away from you?" she says with a fierceness to her voice I did not think was possible. It almost takes me aback -- almost.

"Oh, but what about Zach?"

"What about him?" she retorts, obviously annoyed.

"Wouldn't you lose him without the dreams?"

"That will never happen."

"You sound so sure," I whisper.

"I am."

"Oh, but that's where you're wrong, my girl." She actually cringes when I say this. "You will lose him. Soon."

"Get out of my head!" she yells in my face.

"All you have to do is wake up," I taunt. She cannot wake up now, she is too deep in this dream, too close to REM. But, you see, when she is just on that border, the edge of REM, her mind is almost paralyzed, frozen. I can tell this is where she is now. This is right where I want her, where I had her for days in her coma.

"I -- I can't," she stutters.

"What a shame."

"Let me go! How are you keeping me here?"

"I'm not doing anything. It's all because of that messed-up little brain of yours," I tell her and stroke her hair.

She shudders and tries to walk away, but I catch her by the arm.

"Let me go, Mitch!"

"You listen to me. Tell me what happened to Carrie that year or I swear I will--"

"I DON'T KNOW!"

I just stand there, tightening my grip on her arm.

She steps closer, getting in my face. "Why do you care so much about my aunt, Mitch?"

There is this smirk on her face. I want to smack it off. I let go of her arm and turn around.

"Why, Mitch?" she asks again.

What has gotten into this little brat? Who does she think she is, challenging me?

"What did she do that was so bad?" she says, her voice growing stronger with every word.

There is that smirk again. She knows something.

I grab hold of her arm again. "Let's cut to the chase," I suggest. "I know that you know something."

The smirk falters. Her guard fades for just a second, and I see it, clear as day in my mind. The dream-sharer finally did something good with her powers.

"What is that? A diary?" I ask.

"What are you talking about?"

"That book you were just reading."

She looks all around us and gives a fake laugh, "Really? Mitch, there are no books. I think you're losing it."

"I am in your head, stupid girl."

She does not say a word. *Got her.*

"They're Carrie's, aren't they? She was always scribbling in those things."

"So, what if they are?"

In a flash, I have her up against the wall. I really have become my father. "TELL ME," I roar. "What's in the journals?"

I know I need to take it up a notch. Clearly, she is not as afraid of me as she used to be. I let my eyes glow red. She tries to look away, but she cannot.

I can feel the glow almost burning her eyes; she can feel it in her mind.

She cries out in pain.

"Tell me now."

"They're all about you!"

I almost have to laugh. A little bit of pain, and she crumbles like a house of cards.

"Oh, are they?"

"Yes! I know you were with her," she says in an accusing way. "I know you loved her. I know she broke your heart--"

"She did not break my heart--"

"And I'm sorry about that, but I can't fix that. I can't take back what she did or how you found out. I can't change the past."

"She did not break my heart," I repeat. Her eyes have this sad look to them, like she thinks I am pathetic or something.

"She's so different now," she tries to justify. "You don't have to do this."

"You think I'm doing all this because of some girl I dated in *high school?*"

"Yes, isn't that it? You wanted the perfect life, the dream life, with her, and you didn't get it."

"You know nothing. Nothing," I say, stepping away from her. Carrie was not the only problem I had when I was Addison's age. Not even close.

I am tired and I want another beer. So I let her mind slip away and wake myself up from this dream, only to slip into another.

30
- Mitch -
Thursday, December 25th, 1997

Christmas morning. It does not seem like Christmas though. Meg is sleeping in, she had a rough night last night. There are no Christmas decorations, no presents. Mom always did that.

Mom has been in The Haven for about a week or two so far. Who am I kidding? I know exactly how long she has been there: 10 days, 4 hours, and 10 minutes.

I hate that we did that to her. It makes me hate my dad, too. Why couldn't he take care of her here? Why couldn't he just let me? She will not be okay in The Haven, there is no way.

I just wish there was a way to help her.

I look out the front window and notice the thick blanket of snow that coats the front yard.

Meg used to love the snow when we were kids. Now she does not seem to care.

I wish there was something to make her care, something to give her purpose in life. She needs

something to hold on to so she doesn't turn out like
Mom.

I have heard, from Carrie -- who heard from a
relative - that, for dreamers, we really only have two
options in life.

The first option is that we completely and
totally lose our minds. They say you slowly go crazy.
I have heard rumors that half of The Haven patients
are dreamers like me.

The second option is that you leave the dream
realm behind. No one knows how it happens or if it is
even true. It is just a rumor floating around out
there. Supposedly, it is possible to get rid of
dreams. Carrie says she is going to figure it out
someday. But we hear it changes you, that you lose
your memories with the dreaming capabilities.

You dream too much or not at all. I think either
way you would go crazy.

I realize that Mom must have bought Meg some
Christmas presents before things got bad. She always
used to be a planner.

So, I climb the stairs and ease open the door to
my parents' room.

Dad's not here.

It is Christmas morning and my dad is not even
home to see his kids. Where else could the man be? I
figure he is passed out in a bar somewhere in town.

I check the closet first, her typical hiding
place.

Nothing.

I walk over to her vanity and try one of the
drawers.

It is locked, but I do not see a lock on it.

I try the center drawer. It opens right away. *Ah-
ha!*

I pull that center drawer all the way out, tug on
the drawer I had just tried to the right, hear a
click, and the drawer pops open.

It has some makeup inside and some of my mom's
jewelry.

I try the next drawer down.

There is an envelope addressed to my father in delicate, scripty handwriting I had never seen before.

It has already been opened so I decide there is no way I could get in trouble or that he would even notice. So I carefully slide the folded papers out of the envelope.

I am immediately hit by the smell of perfume.

Where did that come from? I wonder, looking around.

I sniff the paper and envelope. *Gross. Why does this smell like perfume?*

I unfold the pages, and from the first line I know what this is.

It is a love letter.

To my dad.

And it is certainly not from my mother. My mother's name is not Judith. She does not write in cursive. This is not a letter from her.

I open the drawer below, realizing that since my mom has been so out of it lately, my dad could hide anything in here and she probably wouldn't look or even find it.

In the next drawer I find a whole stack of letters. They date back pretty far.

All from "Judith".

I never knew I could hate someone I had never met.

I never thought I could hate my own father more than I already did. *He has been cheating on my mother? For two years?*

I try to think back to when my mom's dreams got bad. About a year and a half ago. I wonder if she knew, somehow. Maybe she found out, and that was when she let her dreams take control of her.

I hope she already knows. Because if she does not, this information might just be enough to make her truly go insane.

How could he do that? How did I not figure this out sooner? Why doesn't he just leave then?

Soon I cannot control the anger inside me. I need to do something, go somewhere, run away, punch something, punch him, punch "Judith", whoever she is.

I guess I decide to punch something.

The next thing I know there is a shattered mirror in front of me, tiny shards falling all over the front of my mother's vanity. Blood dripping down my knuckles.

But I do not feel it.

I do not feel a thing.

I almost have to chuckle. *Merry Christmas, huh?*

31

- Addison -
Wednesday, January 7ᵗʰ, 1998

I look all around me. Everything is coated in that same grey haze again. I must have dreamed back to another memory from the journals.

I notice a clock on the wall in front of me. What time is it? Why can't I read the clock? It's like the numbers are all out of order or written in another language.

There's a knocking sound. I turn in the direction of the sound and see a door with some boyband poster taped to the back of it.

"Care-bear, come on, let me in," a voice pleaded from outside the door. I recognize the voice instantly. Mom.

"Go away, Annie!" The shout comes from this body that isn't mine.

"Carrie, please," Mom begs again.

I don't say anything. I try to, but the words just don't come. I cross my arms over my chest, popping a hip out to the side. But no one can see me, so I don't know why I do that.

"Carrie, it's been a week. At least let me bring in some dinner. It's really good! Mom made roast and potatoes. You love roast and potatoes, remember?" Mom's voice reminded me of when I was little and would throw a fit or when I had a bad day at school and would shut myself in my room.

I uncross my arms and take one step toward the door. Then Carrie must've thought better of it and instead flopped on the bed. "Not now, Annie. Roast can't fix this. Leave me alone!"

"No. I'm not going to leave you alone. You're my little sister." It is silent for a minute before my mom speaks again, "Please let me in."

Suddenly tears are flooding down my face-- well, Carrie's face, I guess. I can't seem to do anything to make it stop.

I hear clicking noises, and then suddenly my mom comes rushing in the room.

"How'd you get in?" I ask between sobs.

She wiggles a bobby pin in front of my tear-stained face with that look on her face she gets when she knows she's right.

Then she wraps her arms around me and holds me while the tears flow.

Finally Carrie stops crying and my Mom is able to get her to talk. I don't have any control over what is said, so I just listen carefully, trying to find clues to what date this is.

"It's so bad, Annie."

"What is?" my mom asks, rubbing a hand on my back.

"Everything. My life."

Mom runs a hand through her hair, which I notice is curlier than it is now. She also has this weird mauve lipstick on and her eyes are lined in dark pencil. It's kind of funny seeing a teenage version of Mom. She looks so different, but she seems the same -- confident, put-together, calming, nurturing, even just in the way she cares for her kid sister.

"Tell me," she says in a way that's more asking than demanding.

"The dreams, they're awful. I don't know who's watching them, but someone is. It's like he's trying to change them or something -- change me."

My mom looks rattled by this. "Carrie, what do you mean? Who is watching your dreams?"

"I don't know."

"How do you know someone is?"

"I can feel it. It's like my head isn't the only one. Like there's someone standing over my shoulder all the time."

"Did you tell Mom?"

"No," I say, grabbing a journal that looks like the one I just read off of the nightstand. "Here."

Mom takes the book from my grasp. This book has a red ribbon tying it together. I make a mental note to read the red one next.

Mom sits there, skimming the pages. Her face growing more and more worried with every word she takes in.

"Oh, Carrie," she mutters every few minutes.

It's like Carrie couldn't tell her, couldn't work up the courage to say the words out loud. Maybe that's why she journals, so she feels like she has someone to talk to about all of this.

Finally Mom closes the notebook and looks up. "What can I do?" she asks, her mind clearly spinning with worry and thoughts of how to tackle this problem.

"Give this to Mitch."

We both look down at the envelope I've just handed to her. What's in the envelope? I wonder.

"Carrie, I don't know if he's going to take it."

"Can you blame him if he doesn't? I was horrible to him! But I have to try something. I need to talk to him."

"Okay, I'll try to talk to him and give him this. But just so you know, he hasn't been at school lately either."

"What?"

"Neither has Meg. His mother was in the hospital a few weeks ago. Rumor has it she's been moved to The Haven."

"The Haven?!"

"Apparently." Mom turns away, thinking, then looks back. "Is his mother a dreamer, too?"

"Yes."

"Hmm...What about Ben?"

"He's a dirtbag."

"Well, that's obvious. But what about you and Ben?" my mom asks, not in a girl-talk kind of way, but in a you-better-give-me-a-reasonable-answer way.

"I haven't called him back. And I'm not going to. I feel like he made all of this worse somehow."

"Carrie, I love you, you know that. But you really changed these past few weeks. It's like I didn't even recognize you sometimes."

I don't say anything. *Say something!* I beg. But, of course, I have no control over anything in this dream.

"Come out and eat something," Mom suggests.

"Not hungry."

"Then at least come out and watch a movie with me. I miss my sister. I miss the old Carrie."

"Yeah, well, so do I."

My mom seems to think about that for a minute. Then she stands and kisses Carrie's forehead.

Once she leaves the room, I grab the red-bowed journal again, turning to the next blank page.

My hand scribbles furiously across the page. I watch as curly letters seem to dance onto the pages. I've always loved my aunt's handwriting; it looks like it belongs to a princess.

I catch some of the words as the pages turn and more and more words completely fill the blank spaces.

As the pages turn, I read these words and phrases:

I'm not myself.

I need to do something, fix this. How can I fix this?

Crazy.

The Haven

Dreams or nightmares?

All I think about is him.

How did I let him slip away? Or, I guess, why did I push him away?

I love him. But it's too late.

Who is Carrie Moore?

Then the pages stop turning, and just as the dream begins to go out of focus, I read the last few sentences Carrie wrote.

If he won't take the letter from Annie, I'll just dream myself into one of his dreams. It wasn't too hard to dream myself away that one time Mitch helped me. He's been teaching me tricks like that, ways to escape whoever is watching my dreams. He helped me that time, but how hard could it be? I'll just dream my way to him, and then he'll have to listen to me.

So, she can dream to other places, too, and so can Mitch, I realize just as everything fades to black.

32

- Addison -
Tuesday, December 20th, 2016

*W*hen I woke up from the past, I had my head resting on Zach's shoulder while the credits of the movie I just slept through rolled up the TV.

I yawned and rubbed the sleep from my eyes.

"Wow, I slept through that whole thing!" I said in my I-just-woke-up voice.

Zach didn't say a thing; he just fidgeted a little.

"Was it any good?" I asked, fidgeting a little myself, trying to get closer.

I felt his arms go around me tighter. He gently sat me up and edged over, further away from me on the couch.

Okay, what just happened here?

"Zach, I know you love that movie, and I'm sorry. We can watch it again sometime, and I promise I'll stay up. I was just really tired today and --"

"Where'd you go? Just now." He finally looked at me, but only because he was searching my face for answers.

"What are you talking about? I took a nap," I lied.

"Ad, come on. I know you. You're a dreamer; you never just 'take a nap'."

I sat up a little straighter. I couldn't tell him. Not yet anyway. It was too new. I sighed. "No where. It was just a dream."

"Don't lie."

"I didn't!" I said defensively.

"Yes, you did. I can tell." He paused. "Wanna know how?"

"How?" I asked.

"You were holding my hand when you fell asleep. You wouldn't let go."

"Oh," I said with a sigh, thinking how cute it is falling asleep on him.

"Ad."

"What?"

"Did you forget your powers?"

"My powers? Really, Zach?" I chuckled.

"You're a dream sharer."

"Yeah, I know." I rolled my eyes. *Such a great power, huh? Sharing my pain with other people.*

He turned so he faced me square on. "Yes, so if you're a dream sharer and you fell asleep holding my hand..."

I gasped as I realized what he meant.

"Why didn't you tell me you could do that?" he asked. He looked really angry.

"Oh, please, you knew I could share dreams when you met me! You're the one who explained it all to me. All dreamers have natural-born powers. I'm one of the lucky ones, a dream sharer! Remember?" I said sarcastically.

He just stared at me.

"You can make people dream of their happy place or whatever. I thought those would go away after I woke up from that coma; I thought the powers were a part of that long dream, something made up. But clearly the dream sharing thing is real. What's the big deal?"

"That wasn't your dream."

"Huh?"

"That dream you just showed me. It wasn't yours. It wasn't even in our dream realm."

"Zach, I was going to tell you. I just didn't know how." I looked away.

"Why would you do that, Addison? Why would you go into another person's dream?"

He never calls me "Addison;" it's always just "Ad."

"I don't know... it just happened. Then I just had to know what was happening to me. I fell asleep while reading her journal, and, I don't know, I just...I need answers, Zach," I told him, pleading.

"But to go and do that? Really? You know it's not safe to do that." The look on his face just then was what scared me the most. It was like I betrayed him, or like I was some little kid he had to always keep an eye on or I'd get hurt.

And that made me mad.

"I know what I'm doing, Zach," I told him defiantly. *This is my power,* I thought.

"Do you? Because if you did, you wouldn't have put your life at risk like that." He shook his head. "Why'd you lie?"

"I don't know. I was worried you'd act like this!"

"Like what? Trying to protect you? Addison, you know this whole dream thing is way more serious than it seems. Why would you go into another person's dream realm without telling me? I wouldn't know how to find you."

"Zach..." I let his name hang in the air, not sure what I was supposed to say next.

"You don't get it, do you?" he asked, clearly still angry.

"Yes, Zach. I do get it. I understand how dangerous these dreams are, and that's why I'm trying to find a way to get rid of them."

"You could've done it a different way." He gave me a look. Silence.

He took a breath, "What did you find out?"

"Well, not nearly enough. Not yet anyway. But, Zach --"

"Just stop." He stood up now and walked across the room. "Don't go back there, Ad. You're playing with fire."

He said "Ad" again. It would be okay. I didn't even listen to his warning to me. All I could hear was the softness creep back into his voice.

"Zach, look," I stood up and walked over to him. "I know you just want to protect me, and I love knowing that you'd do anything, but this is just something I need to do." I reached for his hand.

Please don't pull it away, I thought.

He didn't, so I took hold of his hand and we stood there like that for a minute, neither of us knowing quite what to say.

He breathed out a heavy sigh, "Fine." He pulled me a bit closer and added, "But I'm going with you next time."

"Okay."

* * *

Later that night, I sat in bed thinking of what period in time I wanted to try to dream back to next. *Should I skip a while and see what Carrie was like a year later? Should I go back in time and see what her first bad dream was like?*

Before Zach left he made me promise to bring him with me next time I jump between dream realms, which apparently is a whole other power that typically takes a long time to master. He actually seemed pretty impressed I had done it by accident, but also a little jealous.

He told me that he had tried that when he was younger, trying to go back to dreams his mom had or even just memories of them. He said Mitch had been showing him ways to switch realms, and that's when they found my dreams, I guess.

Just then there was a knock at my bedroom door. It was open just enough that I could see my mom's bright pink sweatshirt that she wears once she's in for the night.

"Hey, Mom," I said with a smile.

"Hey, kiddo," she replied, a hint of sadness coating her voice. "May I?" she asked, pointing to my bed.

I slid over so there was room for her, too. She crawled up next to me, and I snuggled into her, feeling like a little kid again.

"So, listen. I've been wanting to talk to you about something," she started.

"What's up?"

"Well, you see, Dr. Hardy...she was in my class back when I went to Madison."

"Oh, really? I never knew that," I told her, sitting up a little straighter as I realized this was probably going to be a serious talk.

"Yeah." Mom sat there for a while, thinking. I let her go, knowing that she would talk once she had formed her thoughts.

About a minute later she sighed, "This has been a little strange for me, quite honestly. She's the third student from my class to pass away so young. First Jerry, then Meg, and now her. It just makes you think about life, ya know?"

I nodded. *Meg, as in Zach's mom,* I thought.

"Anyway, I wanted to take this opportunity to make sure you know how much I love you. And how much your father loves you, too."

I smiled, "I know, Mom. I love you guys, too."

"And your Aunt Carrie," she continued on, "She loves you like a daughter, and I'm so thankful you have her in your life."

"Me, too. I'm really glad she's been here these last few weeks. It's been nice to see her for more than two or three days at a time."

"I agree. I'm hoping she'll start coming around more. I think that being back home showed her how much she really misses it, whether she's willing to admit that or not." Mom must've realized she was getting off track of what she came up here to talk to me about because she shook her head and began again, "Anyway, I just want you to realize how many people you have in your life who love you and support you. We would all do anything for you, you know that. Even Cammie. That girl would give up shopping or her cell phone for you -- and we both know how much she loves those things."

"She would," I said, grinning. *That girl really loved her phone.*

"My point is, no matter how bad you think something is in life, there's always a bright side to it, a silver lining. It may take some searching, but there's always good to come out of any bad situation. Nothing is ever bad enough that you can't tell me or your father or your aunt or Cammie, okay?"

"Okay. But, Mom, where is all this coming from?"

She took a breath. "The whole town's been talking about it. I assumed you already heard."

"Heard what? Mom, what's going on?"

"Dr. Hardy?" When I obviously was still lost, she explained, "They're now saying her death wasn't accidental. I guess she overdosed. Apparently, she'd been struggling with an issue with prescription medication for a while now. Her brother, he was in your aunt's class, tried to get her help, but I guess it didn't work."

I was stunned. Dr. Hardy, the psychiatrist who seemed to have her life together, overdosed? "Wow," was all I could say.

"Honey, listen to me." She turned to face me and took both my hands in hers. "Nothing, *nothing*, is ever that bad. I am always here for you -- we all are. I know high school is tough, and I know your accident complicated things, but I also know that you are beautiful and brilliant, and you have the most compassionate heart of anyone I've ever known. You are so strong, and I just hope that nothing ever breaks you, and no one ever hurts you. And if they do, you need to come talk to me. You'll understand when you have kids someday, but -- you never think you can love someone more than life until you hold your baby for the first time and know that you would do anything to protect them. So this is me trying to protect you, trying to keep you strong and brilliant and beautiful for as long as I can. Please know that I love you to the moon and back, and that there is nothing so bad in this world that will ever separate us."

Her eyes were blurred by the tears threatening to spill over and turn into waterworks.

"Thanks, Mom. I love you to the moon and back," I said as she smoothed my hair and bit back the tears.

"Now get some sleep. Goodnight. Sweet dreams, Addison Grace," my mother told me, tucking me in like she always used to when I was little.

33

- Mitch -

Monday, December 19th, 2016

I wake up and look around. I am lying on the ground in front of the recliner in Bill's place. I am breathing heavy, trying to calm myself. It felt so real. That dream felt so real this time, like I was back there again.

And just like that, the anger comes rushing back. I hate my father for what he did, and I hate myself for letting it happen.

Then the front door slams closed.

"Hey!" I call out.

No answer.

I get up and walk out into the hallway where Bill is bent over, untying his shoes.

"Bill?" I ask.

"Go away."

"Come on," I try.

"I said 'go away,' Mitch."

"Wow," I say under my breath.

"Wow?" he asks. "My sister just died, Mitch. I just buried her, just now. And you have the nerve to 'wow' me?"

I do not say anything; I just turn and head toward the kitchen.

"You should've been there, Mitch," he calls out after me. "You're my best friend. You should've been there."

Silence.

"She loved you, you know," he tells me. It is not a question. He knows I know that. I have known since the ninth grade. It still baffles me that anyone could ever love me. Maybe back then, sure, but certainly not now.

"You should have been there for her."

"She couldn't have loved me," I say, even though I know that is not true. I knew she would do anything for me, so I took advantage of that. A lot.

Bill laughs, which surprises me. But then I realize he is not laughing because he finds something humorous. He is doing that thing where he just starts laughing when he is incredibly mad or stressed or when he has been awake for more than twenty-four hours.

"Bill?" I ask, honestly a little scared of him in this state.

"She loved you. But I hate you. I'm done helping you. I don't even know why I do. I'm out."

"What are you saying?"

"I'm saying get out of my house. Leave. We are done here. Find a new yes-man."

He cannot do this, not now. Not when we are so close.

"Bill, that's not wise. You need me."

"I don't need you. In fact, I'd be better off without you. Just like Sandy would have," he says angrily.

"Exactly. Look at Sandy. Don't you get it? You are a dreamer just like her. All dreamers go crazy at some point, Billy-Boy. It's only a matter of time."

Bill looks at me funny, like he is confused.

"You're next." And with that, I walk right out the front door and keep walking until I reach the apartment I had been living in with my nephew when we moved back to Madison a few months ago.

When I get there, the door is unlocked and cracked open just a bit. I walk inside and look around.

I am half expecting to find Zachary inside, but he is nowhere to be found. The place looks like no one has been living there in a long time. It is completely empty, like a ghost town.

I wonder for just a second where the kid has been living and if he is okay. Only for a second though.

34

- Addison -
Thursday, December 22nd, 2016

*A*fter school today, Zach drove me home. It was officially Christmas break, and I was so excited to have the two weeks off. I found a radio station with some pop songs from the '90s and turned the volume up all the way.

"Oh, no! Not '90s pop!" he cried.

"Oh, yes! Yes, '90s pop!" I cheered.

The chorus started, and I didn't even try to hide my horrible singing voice from him at all. I never really sang in front of anyone, just usually in the shower or in the car. The fact that I actually started singing in front of my *boyfriend* shocked me. But it was too late to turn back, so I sang at the top of my lungs, terribly, I might add, and he just laughed as he drove.

"Ohhhhh," I sang.

He turned his head and a wide smile spread across his face. He shook his head and looked back at the road again.

"What?" I asked as the songs were changing. "Oh my gosh! I love this one!"

He laughed again.

"What?"

"Nothing. You're just such an incredible singer!" he said, an edge of sarcasm to his tone.

"I used to want to be a singer."

"Oh, really?" he asked skeptically.

"Yup. This song was my jam. I would play it on my little CD player and practice my singing, pretending I was on a stage. I even had dances made up for it, too."

"Wow. Now you've got to show me the whole performance."

"Never!" I told him, just as the chorus started up again.

I sang the rest of the song, and it finished just as we pulled into my neighborhood. I reached over and lowered the volume.

"Oh, come on, sing one more! Encore!" he joked.

"Oh, please! You're glad it's over."

"No, I liked seeing you like that."

"Like what?"

We came up to my driveway. He pulled the car in and turned it off. "Just...I don't know, like you didn't have anything to worry about. You were having fun," he said turning to face me.

"I always have fun around you," I said, as if that was enough to say about how I felt around him. And it wasn't. I felt happy, fun, pretty, nervous (a good nervous), and so many other things, but most importantly, I felt like I could be myself. I didn't feel like I had to hide any part of me from him. *He knows about my crazy dreams and hasn't already run for the hills, so why couldn't I be my bad-singing self around him?*

"I always have fun around you, too."

"Zach?"

"Yeah?"

"Thank you."

"For what?"

For what? For always protecting me, for laughing at my bad singing, for letting me be myself, for helping me with the dreams. "For everything," I said, and leaned over, closing the distance between us.

"Anything for you," he whispered, just before his lips met mine.

My eyes closed, and as I breathed in the smell of him, I wondered what cologne he used, because whatever it was, it was making me dizzy -- in a good way! -- . I slipped a hand around his neck, and he moved closer to me. I could tell he was smiling as my lips moved against his.

I was twisting -- somewhat awkwardly, might I add -- in the front seat of his car, trying to get even just a smidge closer to this boy who had a way of making my heart beat way too fast. I felt him brush my hair back, and then his palm rested against my cheek.

Knock, knock, knock.

"What was that?" he whispered, pulling away ever-so-slightly.

My eyelashes fluttered open for just a second, and what I saw made me jump.

"What?" Zach asked, looking scared.

I just pointed right behind him. He slowly turned to look out the car window.

A flush of red creeped all the way up his face as he saw who was standing outside his car.

My aunt.

My crazy aunt, standing there smiling and waving at us.

She tapped the window, and he pushed the button to roll it down. "Hi, Ms. Moore," he said in the politest voice I'd ever heard. He swallowed.

"Hello, Zachary. Great to see you again! Beautiful day, isn't it?" she asked, chipper as ever.

"Hi, Aunt Carrie. How are you?" I said, covering my mouth with my hand as if that would somehow help this situation.

"Hello, darling! I'm doing great! I can see *you* are, too," she answered, unable to hide her grin. *She would never let me live this moment down!*

There was a second of awkward silence before Aunt Carrie spoke again, "Well, why don't you two kiddos come help me with the groceries? Your mother should be back from work any minute now. Wouldn't want her to see you two makin' out on my watch!" she exclaimed. I blushed and gathered up my things.

"So, how are things, Zach?" she asked enthusiastically as he grabbed two paper bags of groceries out of the back of her car. I noticed it was parked right behind Zach's car. *I wonder how long she was parked there?* I thought, embarrassment creeping back up my cheeks.

"Pretty good," he said, clearly still unsure where he stood with my aunt.

"And what are your intentions?" she asked, face as straight as ever, but I knew she was joking.

He gulped.

"Relax, boy," she told him as I grabbed a bag full of food myself.

He smiled a small, half-hearted smile and adjusted the way he was holding the bags. He seemed so nervous. It was actually kind of cute! I wasn't used to seeing him this way.

"I meant with school," she clarified. "Any idea what you want to do yet?" We had reached the front door then and stood there as she fished around in her big purse for keys. I didn't even know she had a key to our house.

"I'm not entirely sure yet, but I'm thinking some type of engineering," he replied, sounding a little more confident now.

"Engineering?" I asked, realizing we had never really talked about that. I mean, we were almost halfway through our junior year, but I guess with all the dreams and craziness I never thought to ask him about his career plans. Quite honestly, I hadn't even thought about *my* career plans.

"Uh, yeah. I think it's interesting. My dad's an engineer."

"Well, it's an awesome field to go into!" my aunt said. "Ah-ha!" she yelled as she found the key and successfully unlocked the door.

We walked the groceries in and set them on the counter top. Zach started emptying the bags, already knowing where we kept things like chips and cereal.

"Oh, don't worry about that," Carrie said. "I'll get that all put away. You two go on and study or something."

"Are you sure?" I asked, placing a few items in the freezer drawer.

"Yes, yes. Go! But I will be checking in on you two every two minutes on the dot!"

"Aunt Carrie!" I looked away from Zach so he couldn't see the embarrassed look on my face.

Then her phone rang, and she rushed to grab it, shooing us away.

I grabbed my backpack by the front door, and the two of us went downstairs. As soon as we got downstairs, he put down his books and turned to me. I dropped my backpack and threw my arms around his neck.

"Sorry about that," I said, nodding my head toward the stairs but actually meaning my aunt.

"No worries," he said. "At least that wasn't your dad."

"That's very true!" I bit my bottom lip, not sure what to say or do, and then suddenly remembered the journals. "So..."

"So..." he said, edging a little closer to me.

"I have an idea," I told him.

"What's that?" He had his signature grin plastered on his face as he asked me this.

"My aunt will probably be on the phone for a while, so I was thinking..."

"Yeah?"

I placed my hands on his chest and was almost bouncing with excitement as I told him I had finished the blue journal and that I really wanted to dream back to find out what the red one was all about. His smile faded a little, clearly thinking I would suggest we just kill some time by kissing for a while. But no way was I risking Aunt Carrie walking by again! Or worse: my dad!

"Ad, I don't think that's a good idea," he said, serious again.

"Come on, Zach! You said yourself I had to bring you with me next time I try to jump dream realms."

"I know, but... I don't think you're ready for that."

"Don't you want answers? Don't you want to know what she did to get rid of these dreams? Don't you want a normal life, too?"

"But what if she did something really bad or dangerous to get rid of them? Or what if it erases everything dream-related completely?"

"Zach, I'm not going to do that. I don't want to lose you or our memories. But I can't go on dreaming like this, not forever."

"I just don't know why Mitch is so curious about what she did," he said.

"Well," I started, pulling the stack of journals out of my backpack. "Maybe he wished he could've gotten rid of the dreams, too."

"Not a chance," Zach said, sounding so sure.

"Why do you say that?"

"The dreams give him a sense of power, some purpose. He feels in control. He would never give that up. He always said he felt so powerless and worthless in high school. No way he would give up dreaming."

"Well, he loved her. She broke his heart. He wanted the dream life, and he wanted it all with her."

He took one of the journals out of my hand, the one with the purple ribbon. He turned it over and over in his hands. He didn't open it or start to read it; he just stared at it and didn't say a word.

"All right," he spoke finally. "One dream."

"Thank you! Thank you!" I squealed and kissed him, holding his face between my hands. "All right which journal?"

"Red," he answered. I knew he'd pick that one. Red's his favorite color.

We sat there for the next half hour reading quite a few pages of the red journal. It turned out this journal was written right after she broke up with Mitch. The first couple pages were just her thoughts on all the dreams, what happened with Mitch, what happened with Ben, and what happened to her. She seemed really down on herself, really depressed. It was the total opposite of the cheery aunt I know now.

I skimmed through the journal. It was very sporadic, too. The blue ribboned one had been written in almost daily for a whole month, whereas this journal was not as consistent. It covered basically the rest of her junior year and most entries were of her telling a dream she'd had the night before. They were horrible, terrifying dreams.

And honestly, her dreams sounded a lot like mine.

35

"So how exactly does this work?" I asked, settling into the big couch a few minutes later. We had finished reading and decided to try to dream back in time.

"Well, you can dream yourself into another dream realm, but I can't, so in order for me to go with you, I would have to be sleeping first. Then you dream to me, then bring me back to Carrie's dream realm with you. Mitch tried this once," he explained.

He came and sat down next to me. "Don't let go of my hand, okay?"

"Never," I agreed. *Wow, Addison, can you be any cheesier?* I thought to myself as I took his hand in mine.

We were sitting on the couch, all cuddled up like we were going to watch a movie, and I guess in a way we were. But this movie would be playing in our minds, and this movie could change our lives.

We sat there in silence for a few minutes. I noticed his eyes were closed. But was he asleep yet? How did he fall asleep so quickly?

So I poked his shoulder and whispered, "Are you asleep yet?" real close to his ear.

His eyes remained closed, but a smile appeared on his face, and he laughed quietly. "Not yet," he said.

"Okay," I said and just stared up at him.

After another minute or two, his breathing slowed and his head tilted to the side just a bit. I know I should've jumped into the dream then, but I couldn't help it. I just watched him for a minute -- *and, yes, I realize that may sound creepy.* But -- there's this guy, who's always protecting me, sitting right in front of me, sound asleep and dreaming what I hoped was a happy dream. How could I ever protect him the way he's always protecting me? I couldn't imagine my life without him in it now, and I also couldn't imagine the types of dreams he would have. I realized then, as I watched him drifting off into his own dream realm, that I would do anything in my power to keep him safe. I knew he would do the same for me. And I knew that even if that meant figuring a way out of this messed up dream-life, if we were meant to be like I believed we were, -- we would find our way back to each other.

Everything in this life happens for a reason. Every dream means something, especially in a world like ours. Everyone comes into your life for a reason. I have to believe that this -- what Zach and I have -- is for something greater, a bigger purpose, than just your typical high school love story. There's a reason he found his way back to me after the dream in the fall. There's a reason for all the troubles we've faced. They've made us stronger. I have to believe there's a greater purpose for all this. Because if there isn't, then this life is nothing more than an endless nightmare, weighing us down with fear and hurt and darkness. But if there's a reason that I found him, then it gives me the hope to dream that there is a world beyond my life right now, filled with light and love and hope. I don't know what the reason for all of this is, but I'm going to keep fighting and keep dreaming until I figure it out.

I squeezed his hand a little tighter, letting him know I was there and that I was coming. Then I closed my eyes, drifted off, and dreamed my way to him.

I open my eyes and look all around. There's a brightness to everything, like I am seeing the world in perfect sunlight on a perfect day.

"All right, tour guide," he says, drawing my attention to him. He's standing in the bright lights under a tall apple tree wearing jeans and a red hoodie. "Show me around Carrie's dream realm."

Dream-me walks over to him and takes his hand in mine.

"Where should we go first?" I ask.

He thinks about it for a second, "Let's go to the end of her junior year. We aren't finding much in the beginning of the year that helps us see how she changed the dreams. We kind of know why, but not how."

"So, the middle of the red journal then?" I ask, remembering one of the last entries we had read where she was writing about how she wished it could all go away and that she had an idea.

I look down and wriggle my toes in the bright green, soft grass beneath my feet. Why aren't I wearing shoes? I wonder. But the grass is cool, and it reminds me of a nice spring day with the sky so clear and the grass so fresh and new.

Spring day.

Junior year.

Caroline Moore.

The sun flashes like an explosion right before my eyes. It's bright and blinding. It lights up the entire sky and the whole area around us.

I feel us slipping. "Don't let go!" I yell.

"Never," he answers, and I smile because he's pretty cheesy, too.

A wind comes along and sweeps us up into it. I can see the wind, white wisps standing out compared to the baby blue sky.

And off we go, to what I assume will be a spring day in 1998.

36

- Mitch -
Friday, May 22nd, 1998

I instantly know what day it is in this dream. It is Meg's graduation day.

Except Meg is not graduating today. I do not know if she will ever graduate.

Since Mom's death, Meg has really gone down hill. So have I, but it is different with her. It is like she has nothing to live for anymore, so she is letting the dreams consume her.

She keeps coming in at night and sits on the edge of my bed. She is shaking, and she is terrified, telling me to be careful, to watch out for "them," don't let "them" take her away like they took Mom.

The next day she never remembers any of it. I have asked her before, but she just stares on, confused.

She stopped going to school. For a while I thought she was going. We would leave together or I would drive the two of us there. But by lunchtime she was nowhere to be found. Soon teachers started asking where she was, why she had not shown up that day when I knew she came to school.

I later found out she would leave before the first bell even rang, catch a taxi, or walk back home. She knew my dad would not be home during the day. I guess it was one time she could sleep when no one was home. She always apologized for her dreams. I told her she had nothing to be sorry for. My dad told her that she did.

I barely speak to my father, and when I absolutely have to, I say the bare minimum and walk away.

For a while I tried to get Meg to go back to school. But at a certain point, I just could not handle the tears anymore. I did not want to be the one to make her cry. My father did that enough. Her dreams did that enough, too.

After a while I started bringing some of her homework in to her teachers when she asked me to. When she stopped doing the homework, I did a few assignments for her, making sure to get them in on time.

But I have never been as smart as Meg, even on her worst day. So she was still failing.

Then I started failing. The world was catching up with me. I could not spend any more time on her work and still get mine done.

One day the principal pulled me aside in the hallway, "Mr. DeMize, I am sorry to have to do this, but if your sister does not start showing up to class and turning in her assignments soon, she will not be graduating in May."

May was only a few months from that day. There was no way I could turn her grades around.

It was too much, all of it. That day, I went home and tried to drown out the rest of the world with a bottle of alcohol from the back of the cupboard. I did not think my dad would miss it.

Today, I am standing in line at the mini mart in town. The pack of cigarettes trembling in my hands. I am stressed, and it has been too long.

Finally, the slowest possible human being ever rings up my cigarettes and gives me my change, and I bolt out of there. I round the corner of the building, then stop. Leaning back against the brick wall, I take one out and light it.

I look up.

There she is. Just standing there watching me.

Caroline Moore.

Still looking beautiful as ever. Clearly back to her old self, no longer the "emo"-- dressed-in-all-black-makeup-wearing version she has been the past few months.

I have not seen her in months. I have avoided her at all costs at school (when I bother to show up). I do not say a word.

"Hey, Mitch," she offers up, trying to start a conversation.

I nod.

"Look, I know you hate me, but if you could just let me explain --"

"There's nothing to explain, Carrie."

"Mitch, don't be like that," she says, looking down at the ground.

"What do you want, Carrie?"

"Mitch, I'm sorry." Her eyes are pleading, the blue not quite as bright as usual.

I take a long drag of the cigarette.

"Well, I'd better go. I've got to grab a card for Annie. See you at the ceremony?" she asks.

"Meg isn't graduating, Carrie," I say, -- wondering how she couldn't know. It is a small school.

She claps her hand over her mouth. "Oh, my gosh, Mitch. I'm so sorry. How's she doing?"

"How do you think?" I ask, getting angrier with every second this girl stands in front of me. "You of all people know what it's like."

"Maybe I could come talk to her," she suggests.

"And say what?"

She closes her eyes, takes a breath, then continues talking, "And say that I've been doing a lot of research. They say there's a cure. I'm going to go find it. Maybe she could come with me."

"Go with you where?"

"India."

"India? Carrie, you've never even left this town," I say, almost choking on the puff of smoke at how crazy that idea is.

"It could help her!" Carrie says defensively.

"There's no way you're going to India," I say.

"I am. I leave next week."

"How could you leave next week?" I ask. "Seniors are done, but we aren't."

"I got my GED."

"You what?"

"Look, Mitch, I've really got to go. Annie will freak if I'm late. I really hope you'll tell Meg to give me a call or at least let me come over. I think she needs this. I know I need this. I can't go on like it is right now. I just can't. I'm going to get rid of them."

I do not say anything. I just stand there, looking at her -- at my Carrie.

But then I remember she is not my Carrie anymore.

She says goodbye and walks into the mini mart.

I let my cigarette fall to the cement, stomping on it with the sole of my shoe.

I look up and into the window of the mini mart. Carrie is standing in front of the section of cards where there are only about three to pick from.

A kid I recognize from the senior class walks up behind her, reaching out to take a card. They reach for the same one at the same time. She smiles and tosses her hair back.

I turn, kick the garbage can beside me, and walk home, already feeling the need to light another one.

37

- Addison -
Friday, May 22nd, 1998

*E*verything around me is hazy again, like the whole scene is covered in a light fog. But I can tell where I am. I'm in my mother's old bedroom at my grandparents' house. I can tell because the walls were painted hot pink and the wood trim had been painted black.

I'm standing in front of a mirror. The girl looking back at me is not me; she is my Aunt Carrie when she was my age. Her reddish, brownish hair is down to the middle of her back, which is much different than the shoulder length cut she's had ever since I've known her.

My eyes -- or rather her eyes -- are watery with tears.

I'm wondering what day this is, or what is going on right now to make her cry.

I look around and don't see Zach anywhere.

"I'm right here," he says.

I turn. "Where?" I ask when I still don't see him.

"In your mind. I can see everything you're seeing," he tells me.

Involuntarily, I reach out and pick up something white from the top of the bed. I unfold the silky fabric and hold it up in front of me, tilting my head to the side to look at it.

It's a gown. A graduation gown.

I glance back at the bed and see a cap there, too, inside a plastic bag. On the front of the bag is a label that reads: *Anne Moore*.

Tears pour down my face, and I stand there staring at the reflection. I realize then what's going on. Carrie's a junior right now, so she's probably sad my mom was graduating and leaving.

Carefully, without telling myself to do so because this is a memory dream that I have no control over, I lay the gown back over my mom's bed, smoothing it over. *Don't cry, Carrie,* I think. *Mom won't leave Madison forever.* I try to tell my aunt, knowing that my mother stayed in the area.

Then I walk down the hall to Carrie's room. My hand reaches for that red journal again, turning to the very last page.

"Zach," I say in my head, hoping he will hear me.

"Yeah, Ad?" he answers.

"Did we read the very last page?" I ask.

"Not yet."

"I feel like this is going to be important. There has to be a reason we are here in this dream."

The pen I'm holding runs over the page, filling it with words. But I can't read any of them. *Why can't I read any of them?*

After the page is filled with words, I feel angry -- very angry. The next thing I know, the book is flying across the room, slamming into the door of the closet and falling to the ground.

The tears come harder now, and I'm full-on sobbing.

38

- Addison -
Thursday, December 22ⁿᵈ, 2016

I snapped open my eyes and sat up straight. I turned to Zach who was sitting beside me and just woke up himself. "What happened to her?" I asked him, knowing that it had to be something more than being sad that my mom was graduating.

"It has to be in the journal!" Zach said, jumping up and grabbing the journal with the red bow off the table on the other side of the room.

He flipped quickly to the very last page and began to read aloud, "Today totally sucked. I ran into Mitch outside of the mini mart today, and he was horrible. He acted like he didn't even care about me. I guess he has every right to do that; I was awful to him. But still, I guess I thought he would still be there for me. I know that's wrong of me. But he said forever; he promised me forever. And I know I'm the one who broke that promise. But I really think I can fix these dreams, and I'm going to need his help."

I interrupted Zach, "Whoa, fix the dreams? Does it say how? What did she do?"

"Ad, let me finish," Zach replied, laughing at my impatience.

"Sorry!" I bit the inside of my cheek to keep from talking again.

"I leave next week for India. I've been reading up on healing, spiritual and mental healing. I also read this book where the woman had horrible nightmares -- sounds like me, huh? And she went to this town in India and met with some healer who helped her. I've been doing research, and I think I know where to find him. I've been trying to meditate every day until the trip. Oh! And I finally got my GED, so I never have to waste another day in school, sitting in boring classes that will never help me, will never heal me."

"She got her GED?" I asked him.

He continued reading, "Today Annie graduates from Madison High. I'm happy for her, I am. But I will never have that. I'll never be a normal teenager like her. I won't walk across the stage to get my diploma. The way the dreams have been lately I know I won't make it another year of high school -- still sane -- if I don't do something about it. I'll end up like Meg DeMize, alone and scared. I can't live like that. I know it's risky to just hop a plane and go to a foreign country, but what other choice do I have? I really hope this works and --"

"What do you think you two are doing down here?!" Aunt Carrie yells from the stairs, looking down at me sitting on the couch, intently listening while my boyfriend reads her personal journal she thought was thrown away.

I leaped up and ran up next to her.

"Ms. Moore," Zach tried.

"Don't." Carrie's face was stone-cold as she looked at Zach, silencing him. She turned back to me, betrayal showing in her blue eyes.

"Aunt Carrie --" I began.

"I threw those away. Those stupid journals. Addison Grace, what made you think it was okay to read my personal journals?"

"I had to know what happened! You won't tell me anything. You never talk about it. You know I'm going through exactly what you went through and yet anytime I try to ask you about high school or dreams, you conveniently can't talk about it. You wouldn't help me, and I thought reading your journals would give me answers." I was crying then, but I couldn't stop it.

"That's not a reason to do that."

"I know. I'm sorry. But you --"

"Don't you dare make this my fault. *You* took my personal thoughts and words, and you read them. I should've gotten rid of those a long time ago. I can't believe --"

"What's going on down here?" my mother's voice asked as she slowly crept down the steps, trying to assess the situation.

" *Your daughter* has been reading *my* journals from high school with her *boyfriend* after I threw them away. She took them and has been reading them out loud." She turned to me, "Why can't you two just watch a movie or something?"

"Addie?" my mom asked, looking me in the eyes.

"She threw them out. I didn't think she'd care. I needed answers."

"Addison, you should have asked her for permission," my mother chided. As she said this, Aunt Carrie was nodding in an I-told-her-that-already way.

"How could I? She won't ever talk to me about this stuff!"

Then I remembered Zach was standing there, watching all of my family drama go down.

My mom must have remembered then, too, because she turned to Zach and said, "Zach, could you give us a bit? Addison can call you later tonight."

"Yes, ma'am," he answered politely, setting the journal back down on the table as gently as possible, as if that would help the situation, and then he quickly went up the stairs and out of the house.

My mom turned back to me, "Addison, I can't believe you would do such a thing. This isn't like you."

"I know, and I'm sorry." I looked at my aunt, "and I'm so sorry for reading your private, personal thoughts. I just didn't know what else to do. I need you, Aunt Carrie. You're the only one who knows what this is like."

"That's no reason to..." she trailed off and then turned on my mom. "Annie, aren't you going to do anything about this?"

"Like what?" my mother asked.

"Like what?" Aunt Carrie repeated incredulously. "I don't know! I'm not the mom here. Ground her, take her phone away, do something."

"Carrie," my mom began in a calm tone. "I know you're upset. I'm disappointed, too. But why don't we sit down and talk about this."

"*Sit down and talk about this?* You're joking, right?" I could feel the tension building.

"No. I'm not. I really think that's best," Mom replied.

"Sit and talk about what, exactly? How your bratty daughter betrayed me?"

"Excuse me?!" my mom yelled. "*My daughter* is hurting. She needed her aunt. You came here and begged me to let you stay the whole month because you thought you could help her. Why do you think I called you in the first place, Carrie? To just come sit around drinking hot cocoa with her and going down memory lane with me? She needed your help. *I* needed your help. It kills me that I have to watch Addison struggling with things I can never understand.

"But you, you can understand all of this! More than I ever could. You told me you've been talking to her. But she's saying you haven't told her a thing. She can't go talk to her therapist anymore. She needs YOU, Carrie. You are her aunt, and you need to step up and help her. You had people to help you get through this."

"I think I should go," Aunt Carrie said, turning toward the stairs.

"Carrie, no," my mom said, a fierceness in her voice that made my aunt stop in her tracks. "You always said that you wished Mom would've helped you more. Don't be like mom. Help your niece."

Carrie just looked at my mom; she didn't say anything, but she didn't turn to leave either.

"Now sit down. Neither of you are leaving until you talk," my mom said, pointing to the couch.

We both walked over, neither of us saying a word. I sat and turned to face her.

After a couple minutes my mom said, "Well?"

Aunt Carrie turned to me, "What questions do you have?"

Seriously? I thought. *No information to offer up? How am I supposed to pick a question from the million in my head?*

"Were you in love with him?"

"Who?" she asked.

"Mitch."

"Yes, I was."

"Then why did you hurt him like that?"

She looked like I had slapped her. "I guess I deserved that."

My mom added in from over by the stairs, "You kind of did."

"Anne," Aunt Carrie warned. Then to me she said, "I never wanted to hurt him. I didn't realize what I was doing would hurt him that much. I was selfish. If I knew my choices would cause him to hurt you like he has been, I never would have done what I did. Obviously, I feel partially responsible for the person he is today."

"Carrie, it isn't all your fault. You know things were bad for him at home," Mom said.

"I know, but I didn't make it any better. I should've been there for him...anyway, I never wanted to hurt him, Addie."

"Why were you crying on Mom's graduation day?"

"What?" Aunt Carrie gasped.

"In the memory dream. You were pretending it was your graduation cap and gown, but it was Mom's. Then you started crying."

"Wow, I guess I blocked that day out," she said thinking back. "Probably because I would never have that day."

My mom looked like she was going to cry. "Carrie, I never knew you felt that way. I'm so sorry."

"But you could've had that," I pointed out. "You didn't have to go get your GED. You could've stayed in school."

"No, I couldn't have. I had seen too many kids like me not make it to graduation. I was already going crazy. I had to figure it all out."

"Why did you go to India?" I asked.

"I had heard there was a medicine man there who specialized in dreams and healing people like me."

"Did you find him?" I asked.

"Yes. And he really helped. I think I just needed to get away for a while, learn how to block all the bad dreams out. He showed me how to do that."

"How?" I asked.

"Healing of the mind and soul. Meditation, prayer, yoga. Also, eating healthy, natural things. I finally focused on me, making myself more...whole," she said.

"Did it work?" I asked her.

"Yeah, it did. At least until recently. It's easier to block the past out when you live far away from it. I wasn't trying to avoid helping you, Addie. I guess I was trying to avoid letting that part of my life back in. I was afraid that, if I opened my mind to the dreams again, they would all come back and make my life crazy again."

"Did they?"

"No, I think I did heal on that trip. I can remember the past now, but I don't have to relive it."

"I want to go!" I blurted out.

"What?" Mom and Aunt Carrie asked simultaneously.

"I want to go on the same trip you did, Aunt Carrie. I want to get rid of these dreams too."

"Addie, it changes things," Aunt Carrie said.

"What do you mean?" I asked.

"Well, for starters, I moved away. I couldn't handle being in this town. Then I became a vegan and focused on meditating. I didn't talk to anyone from my past for years. Your mother and I grew apart."

"I can't go crazy; I can't let my dreams rule my life. I can't let Mitch rule my life anymore either," I told them, standing up.

Aunt Carrie looked at my mom who thought for a minute and then said, "All right, fine. But I am not letting you go alone. The world has changed since your aunt went. I'm not letting a seventeen-year-old travel the world on her own, so I will go with you."

"Really?" I cried, hugging her.

"I should've done something to help you sooner, sweetheart. I'm sorry." She turned to my aunt, "What do you say, Carrie? Come with us? We can make it fun! The three of us travelling the globe together. We always used to dream about doing that."

"I can't. This is something you need to do on your own. *But* I will help you plan for it and tell you what I know," Aunt Carrie answered.

"That's good enough for me!" I told her, hoping she'd change her mind and come, but also just happy to have my aunt willing to talk finally.

* * *

Later that night we talked to my dad about the plans, and Carrie told me about where she went when she travelled for that year. We did, however, decide that I would wait until after I graduated from high school. It was only a year and a half; I could wait that long. It gave me more time to plan too. That night before I fell asleep, I researched India and other places around the world known for spiritual healing. And that night, I finally had a good night's sleep, dreaming of a future where I was...whole again.

A week before graduation...

39

- Addison -
Friday, May 18ᵗʰ, 2018

I'm sitting at my little window seat, holding a small, light blue, leather-bound notebook. On the front, four words are etched in: "Always follow your dreams."

By now, almost every page had words scrawled on it. Almost.

There were exactly seven pages left. And there were seven days until I graduate from Madison High. So every day from now until then, I am going to fill this journal up with the dreams I have had and my thoughts.

For the last year and a half I have been writing in this diary. I have always wanted to keep a diary; I've always admired people who do. But I never had the time, and quite frankly, I never personally saw the point. Who would ever want to read about my life?

But reading Aunt Carrie's diaries sparked something in me.

I realized that I had turned to her journals as a source of answers. Sometimes reading about her life just gave me more questions. But other times, it really helped to know someone in this world had gone through what I was going through. So then I thought, what if twenty years from now some young girl needs answers, just like I needed them? What if my words could have an impact on someone, let them know they aren't alone? What if when I'm old and forgetting my past, these journals help me to remember this time in my life?

What if my dreams, my history, my life could make a difference to someone else like Carrie's did for me?

So at the start of the year of 2017, I bought this blue notebook, and have been writing in it almost every day since then. I write down anything I think is important. Sometimes that means it's a dream I had, and sometimes it is something funny that happened at school that day and made me smile.

My upcoming graduation had me feeling a little sentimental, so I began opening the notebook to random pages from the past year and a half, just to relive it all for a minute.

Dear Diary,   **Friday, June 9th, 2017**
Aunt Carrie is moving back here!
After she stayed with us for about a month last year, she went back to her apartment to "clear some stuff up."
She just closed on a town home not too far from my house.
I'm so excited to get to see her more often, especially now that she's somewhat willing to talk about her trip.
I told her I'm planning a trip of my own, and she's really excited for me and said she will help me plan. She says she can't come. But I think it's not so much can't as won't.
Either way, I'm just happy to have her back here and back in my life!
Things will be all right! -Addie

Since that day, Aunt Carrie definitely had helped me with planning for the trip. With her memories, what she wrote in the journals, and the information I got from dreaming back to the past with Zach, we have been piecing together what happened on her trip around the world. She went to India, southern France, and Hawaii. She focused on finding her "zen," blocking out the bad dreams with meditation and a healthier, positive life-style. My trip is going to be slightly different.

I turned to a few pages later in my journal.

Dear Diary,   Saturday, October 7ᵗʰ, 2017

Today was the best day.

I decided what I want to study in college! (I haven't picked a school yet, though.) But I'm surprised I had never thought of it until Mom suggested it to me today.

I've been through so much these last few years, things I didn't think anyone would ever understand, and things I didn't always think I could get through. But I did get through it. I'm still getting through it, every day. Life is hard and confusing and scary, but it can also be really great if you let it.

So...I decided to major in psychology!

And I'm honestly so excited! I just really want to help people, you know? I'm going to focus on adolescent development, because the high school years are tough enough as it is, but then you factor in other things going on, and sometimes it's just unbearable. I realized recently that every single kid in my class has something hard going on in their lives right now. For most of them, I'll never know what that is. No one really knows about my messed-up mind. That's because I've hid it. People would think I'm crazy if they knew what really went on in my life. But I realized a lot of my friends, even close friends probably, feel like they can't talk about what's going on or admit they need help.

So I want to become a psychologist and help teenagers like me figure things out and find peace. I'm not going to be like Dr. Hardy and take advantage of my job, or make the teenagers feel even more alone. I want to be there for them and help them get through the tough situations in life.

So I really hope that this works out! Even if I help one person out of the darkness, I would be so happy!

Wish me luck!

Love, Addison :)

I smiled, remembering the feeling of finally figuring my life out -- at least a little bit. This was written months ago, but I still feel just as excited, if not more excited, to study psychology and have a career dedicated to helping teenagers like me.

I turned the page and saw the date at the top. *Prom.*

Dear Diary,   Saturday, May 12ᵗʰ, 2018
    PROM!
    Tonight was our senior prom. It was so incredible! I know that
probably sounds so cliché, but it was just such a fun night with all my
friends before we all go our separate ways soon.
    I found the perfect dress. I hadn't expected to pick a dress
like it at all, but when I tried it on, I just knew. It was fitted and flowed
out at the knees; it was a bright red satin. I worried it was too flashy,
but Aunt Carrie said, "Go bold or go home, sweet pea!" and my mom
told me that I had grown up so much the past few years, dealt with so
much, that I deserved to stand out in such a striking dress. Also, red is
Zach's favorite color :)
    We all laughed all night long and danced until the end of the
night. After prom was over, half the class went to Jessica's house to sit
around her fire pit. It was so lovely, sitting under the stars, Zach's
hand in mine, laughing with the girl who I never thought I could be
friends with again.
    For one night, time felt almost frozen, like we could all just
stay 18 forever, happy and together, not spread out all across the
country studying different things. For a little while the dreams didn't
bother me. I was just a typical teenage girl with her whole life ahead of
her, whose dreams were all about to come true.
Sweet Dreams!
-Addison

On the opposite page, I had written:

Dear Diary,   Monday, May 14ᵗʰ, 2018

    Cammie and Billy broke up today. They decided they were
just better off as friends. Cam is still really upset though, and I feel so
bad. I'm heading over to her house soon to eat some ice cream with
her. She needs a friend to wallow with, so of course I'm going to be
there! It's so weird though, the idea of her and Billy not being
together anymore. They were together for a year and always seemed
like the perfect couple. I mean, they were practically dating for years
before they made it official last year. I got used to the picture of Billy

with my best friend and the idea of them being together forever. But real life isn't always like it is in the movies.

I know Cammie will be happy again one day. She may be heartbroken right now, but I know she'll find someone who makes her feel so loved and so happy. That's all I can hope for my best friend.

Love always,
Addison Grace <3

40

- Mitch -

Friday, May 18th, 2018

This place is falling apart. I am falling apart. My plan is falling apart. Although I have recently realized I never had that great of a plan to begin with.

All that time my sister yelled and screamed about "them" and the people trying to hurt her in her dreams, I never really believed her. It was not until my mother died and later when everything happened with Meg that I realized she was not lying. It was not just something in her head.

There is a reason they say every dreamer goes crazy.

That reason is "them."

Unless you have something else in this life to hold you back from them, to ground you, you don't stand a chance.

Meg had something for a while, during the few years when things were calm with her: her husband,

Adam, and her son. When she was around them, things were fine.

But then the depression set in and they gave her the pills, and the pills made her crazy, brought all the bad dreams back.

But they will come get you, like they do with everyone. Unless you are one of the lucky ones, like Caroline Moore was, you do not stand a chance.

I got so mad when they took my mother from me. I vowed I would find a way to stop them. I began assembling the dream team of other dreamers like me. I wanted to put a stop to "them," whoever they were, once and for all.

The great thing was that I was always the strongest, the leader. It showed me that if I had to go up against "them," I could. I trained every day. I studied dreams every waking hour. I taught the members of my team, like Bill, Sandy, Jess, Zach, and others, how to dream and control their dreams. I taught them just enough to keep them on my side and trusting me, but never enough that they could all turn against me. I was unstoppable.

But then I could feel it all falling apart when that bratty little Addison came in the picture. That girl has more natural talent in the dream realm than anyone I have ever met or heard of, myself included. And the best part (and the worst part) is that she did not even know how unique she was. I could not let her find out.

Addison Smith would not and will never get in the way of my plans.

I wanted to take "them" down, stop them.

Actually...

I wanted to *be* them. I wanted to be the entity everyone feared. I wanted my name to be great, my legacy to be known amongst dreamers everywhere.

And I told Carrie all of this back in high school, that I wanted to rule the dream realm someday so that neither of us would ever have to worry, so our kids would never have to worry. I wanted everything with her.

But she said no when she did what she did. Then stupid me thought there would still be hope for us, maybe down the road when I became that guy with all the power. But again she said no and made it perfectly clear that she was saying no when she got rid of her dreaming abilities.

I did not know how she did it. It had always just been a rumor in the dreamer world. But she did it. I could no longer locate her brainwaves once she fell asleep. I used to be able to find her dreams easily, but then they got hazy, and one day they were completely gone.

I walk over to the sink, turning on the faucet, letting the low-pressure water run over my calloused hands. Some water gets on the sleeve of my shirt, so I use my other wrist to try to push the sleeve further up my arm. I see all the scars covering my left wrist from my dark days at the end of high school when I tried to drown out the pain with another pain.

I remember the day Sandy came over to see me and was the one to force me to stop doing that. I often think it is ironic that she saved me countless times from hurting myself but no one could save her.

I pat my hands dry on the ratty dishtowel beside the sink.

Let's see, what time is it? I wonder. It is past 11:30, meaning Addison will be asleep by now.

I sit down on the couch, kick my feet up, crack my knuckles, and try to find Addison's mind in the dream world.

Found it. Go time.

I remember a recent dream she had. In it, she basically ran through a mini-movie of all of her fears in life: spiders, snakes, thunderstorms, losing her parents, Zach getting hurt, losing Cammie (either by death or just growing apart), Zach hurting her or not being who he says he is, and, of course, me.

Every night since that dream, I focus on one of her fears, playing thousands of scenarios of how each of those things could happen.

Tonight, we are on the dream about Zach hurting
her. I have been thinking about all of the scenarios I
could use to scare her to the bones.

I start with a dream in which she is back at
Sal's (where she found out in the coma dream that Zach
was my nephew), but this time I twist it a bit.

I have the dream go like this: I come in the
restaurant, call Zach my nephew, Addison is all
shocked and scared, but instead of Zach trying to
smooth things over saying he is all into her and other
crap like that, instead, he picks her up and carries
her right to me.

Another scenario I show her is that Zach's name
is not even Zach. He is not even a high school
student. He has been lying to her about everything.

I can tell Addison's heart rate is picking up.
She is getting scared.

In the next scenario, Zach is dating Jess… or
wait, no, make it Cammie. He has been with Cammie for
months now, and Addison just found out. She is
crushed. Poor thing.

I save the worst for last.

* * *

I can tell the lights are flickering from behind my
eyelids. I open my eyes, trying to figure out what
could possibly be going on. *Did I pay the electric
bill this month?*

When I open my eyes, my nephew is standing there,
flipping the light switch up and down, calling out my
name.

He looks different since I last saw him, older.

"Mitch, what the hell?"

"Good to see you too, nephew," I say, standing up
and walking over to him.

He steps to the side, out of my reach. "This
place is a mess. How do you live like this?"

"Oh, like you care."

"Well, you're still my uncle," he says as if it
is obvious, but at the same time there is a tinge of
anger in his voice that seems to say he has to care
even though he doesn't want to.

"What are you doing here, Zachary?" I spit out.

"I heard from Bill you were back in town. Actually he said you've been back for a while now. I wanted to come see if it was true."

"Where's that girl of yours?" I ask, even though I know she is at home sleeping.

"Addison is fine," he says, crossing his arms, not actually answering my question.

"I wouldn't be so sure about that," I warn.

For a split second he looks scared. Then he fixes his face, cold as stone again.

"What are you doing back, Mitch?"

"No 'Uncle Mitch' anymore? Don't I deserve some respect, kid?"

He laughs, "Respect? No. You lost that from me a long time ago."

"Well," I grind my teeth and set my jaw. "I came back because there's unfinished business here."

"I knew you'd say that," Zach says. I have to admit he seems more mature, and he does not seem as afraid of me. He is standing taller, more sure of himself now, arms crossed like he is not putting up with anything. He takes a step closer and says, "You do not have any unfinished business, Mitch. It's finished. There's nothing you have left to do; you are done. And by the looks of this place, I'd say you're well on your way to losing your mind -- if you haven't already lost it."

"I am not," I yell.

"Look, all I came to say is this: I don't care if you're back. I don't care if you leave again. Just stay away from me, and stay away from Addison. Get out of her head. You and I both know how strong she is, and when she realizes that, she can crush you. So just leave her alone, or you'll have to deal with me."

I pretend to shake. "Oh, wow. I am so scared. Big boy Zach will hurt me if I don't stay away from his precious girlfriend." I smile. "But trust me, you would never hurt me. You couldn't. You just don't have it in you, buddy, and that's okay."

"I could call them, you know," he says.

Now this, does worry me. I try not to let my face show it. "You're bluffing," I tell him.

"No, I'm not. One call to The Haven and --" I let out a breath when I realize he was talking about The Haven, not "them". He continues, "-- you're gone. With you living like this, in this mess, and how crazy you sound, they'll take you away in a heartbeat. In fact, I oughta take you there right now."

Oh, boy, I think, *I have been waiting years for this.*

"Go ahead. Take me there."

"What?" he asks, shocked I am agreeing so easily. I kind of feel bad because what I am about to say, he definitely doesn't see coming.

"Take me to The Haven. Then you can visit your *mommy* after you drop me off there," I say with a twinkle in my eye as his face goes cold.

"My mother died ten years ago, Mitch," he points out.

"No, she didn't."

"Yes, she did!" he yells at me, edging closer.

"I assure you, my boy, she did not die."

"Mitch, I swear, you better stop it right now. My mom doesn't deserve you acting so nonchalant about her death and joking about it. Just stop."

"Zachary, I'm not kidding. When you thought she had died, your father really just admitted her to The Haven."

"You're lying. She was sick. I SAW HER. I HELPED HER. She was sick and she died."

"She was sick, all right. But she was sick in her head, not in the way you thought."

He reaches out and knocks over a lamp that has not been on in a while. The bulb burnt out, and I never replaced it.

"Stop!"

"Want me to prove it?" I ask.

"Yeah, go ahead and prove it. I know you're lying."

"Give me your phone," I say.

He tosses it to me, and I dial the number I know by heart now.

"Hello? Thanks for calling The Haven. How can I help you?" a lady's voice I recognize answers.

"Hi, Patricia. It's Mitch DeMize."

"Oh, hi, darlin'!" she answers.

I put the phone on speaker so Zach can hear the next part.

"I was calling to let you know I'll be in to visit tomorrow, and I wanted to check on my sister."

"Oh great, she'll be so thrilled to see you again!" Patricia says. "Meg is doing just fine, darlin'. She's getting better every day since we started her on that new medication I was telling you about."

"Oh, that's great. Well, tell her I'll be by tomorrow and that she also might get another visitor."

I hang up and toss the phone back at Zach. He barely catches it. He is staring right past me, at nothing.

"Still don't believe me? Go visit her tomorrow. You will see. Your mother, my dear nephew, is very much alive."

He does not say a word. He just yells an unintelligible word and runs out the front door.

41

- Addison -
Friday, May 18ᵗʰ, 2018

I decided to read one last entry before I went to bed. It had been so nice not having homework to do this week (because everything's done!) and having time to read or journal or plan more for our trip. So I curled up under a soft, crocheted, blue blanket sitting on my little window seat. The light from the moon came dancing in through my window lighting up the pages of my journal and making my room appear almost dream-like.

But I wasn't dreaming, not yet anyway. I could read the words on the pages. Something that's more difficult when I'm dreaming. I knew what time it was, which is another thing that's unclear in the dream realm. And for once I could just tell ... I was awake. I could feel it like I could feel the cool pages between my fingers.

Dear Diary,   Monday, September 4ᵗʰ, 2017
So...
Today Zach told me he loved me.

I told him I loved him too. Because I do. I think I've known for a
while but was too afraid to admit it out loud.
But I love him. And he loves me back!
Maybe the good dreams do come true after all...
-Ad

I smiled, remembering that day so clearly. We were off of
school for Labor Day, and it was a really nice day, so we went on a
picnic at a park nearby. We were sitting there on a blanket eating
watermelon (my favorite), when he just started rambling on and on. I
honestly wasn't following his nervous string of words until a few words
caught my attention.

"And I'm not sure if you feel this way, and I don't want to
pressure you into saying anything you aren't ready to say, and, I mean,
I don't want to scare you, but to be honest, it kind of scares me too,"
he said, red creeping up his neck just a bit.

I reached up my hand to cover my mouth so he couldn't see
my grin. Zach was always so sure of himself, so strong, that I loved
these little moments when he let his wall down, let me all the way in.
The fact that he still got flustered around me made me feel so much
better, because I still got nervous around him.

"Zach, what's wrong?" I asked him, sitting up straighter and
setting down my watermelon.

"It's just..."

"Yeah?"

Say it.

"I really, really like you, Addison. Actually, I'm pretty sure I'm
in love with you."

I sat there for a second, letting that thought sink in. I guess I
realized then that I had been wanting him to say those words for a
while. I just couldn't admit them myself.

He picked at a stray string on the blanket. "Or, I guess, I am.
Not 'pretty sure', I mean. I am sure."

He finally looked me in the eyes, his brilliant blues staring into
mine. He seemed a bit more confident, more sure of himself this
time, as he said, "I love you, Addison Grace."

When he said that, there was no containing my smile. "I love
you, too, Zach!" I practically yelled right in front of his face and kissed
him.

* * *

Now, sitting in my room, I pulled the blanket tighter around me and closed my journal. *That was a good day,* I thought, closing my eyes, hoping my mind would just float away to a happy memory like that one. I could live in that dream.

I blink a few times, my eyes adjusting to the sudden brightness around me.

I'm outside, in a park, with bright green grass beneath me and a happy yellow sun shining above me. It worked; I'm dreaming of that day.

But then the scene changes so fast that it makes me dizzy.

I'm sitting on a couch that isn't mine. It's a blue-green color and not very comfortable. I feel like I'm in my basement, but nothing looks right. Then I see Zach walking over toward me. Except he isn't walking toward me, he's walking past me. It's like he doesn't even see me there.

"Zach?" I ask.

Nothing.

"What about Addison?" I hear behind me.

I spin around and there's Cammie, walking toward him.

What about me?

"She doesn't have to know," Zach answers.

What?!

Then, as if in slow motion, they lean in toward each other, and I just sit there watching them get closer and closer.

Please don't, I think. *How could you two do this?*

And then I realize that I must be dreaming. I have to be.

They're about to kiss and I'm about to cry, throw-up, scream, or stomp my foot like a little girl throwing a tantrum.

He's mine! And you're my best friend! I want to yell. *Please be a dream! Wake up, Addison! Wake up!* I yell at myself because I know they can't hear me.

I know this has to be Mitch. There's no way this is real. The only person who could ever think or try to make me think Zach would be with Cammie behind my back is Mitch.

I squeeze my eyes shut tight. *Change the dream, Addison. Go somewhere else.*

Then, in a flash, I'm back in the park, on a picnic blanket, next to Zach, with Cammie nowhere in sight, and a new sense of calm to the dream.

It worked! I think.

Then I woke up.

I bolted upright in bed, trying and failing to catch my breath. I got out of bed and flipped on my light switch.

How did I change that dream? Why couldn't I ever do that before?

I paced back and forth, back and forth across the length of my room.

What if I could just change my dreams when Mitch tried to cut in like that? Zach always said I had more powers than I knew, maybe that's one of them. Maybe I could keep working on this, get stronger, block Mitch out.

My mind was spinning a mile a minute.

Zach. What if there was more to that dream? There's no way he could really be interested in Cammie, right? What if it's not Cammie, but it's someone else? Oh, my gosh, what if there is someone else?

Or what if he's expecting more from me because I told him I love him? But I'm not ready for that.

What if...

Then I heard the doorbell ring.

I whipped my head around, looking at my clock. 12:02. *Who would be here at 12:02 in the morning?*

I crept over to my doorway and listened through the open crack. I heard my dad grumbling about the time of night it was the whole way from the family room, where he no doubt had fallen asleep watching TV, to the front door. He opened it and said, "Zach? Well, this is an odd time for you to be showing up here."

Zach?! I can't see him right now, not with the picture of him and Cam still in my head.

"I'm sorry, Mr. Smith," I heard Zach say. "I really need to see Addison. I know it's late, and I'm sorry. I promise it'll be quick."

"I think she's asleep already," my dad replied. Then, a beat later, "Actually, her light's still on. Hang on. Come on in."

What are you doing, Dad? I yelled in my mind.

A knock came at my bedroom door, and I jumped back. "Addie," my dad whispered, "Zach's here. Are you awake?"

My plan was to not say a word, make him think I was asleep, have him send Zach away and I could deal with all of this later. But, as usual, my plan was ruined because I'm a clumsy human being. I had stepped back and walked into my bookshelf, sending books clattering to the floor.

I went over and opened the door, looking at my dad who was standing there looking tired and confused as to what was going on. "Where is he?" I asked, noticing he wasn't down in the front entry anymore.

"Addison?" Zach asked, stepping around my dad.

"You have five minutes, then you need to leave, Zach," Dad warned.

"Yes, sir," Zach said and walked into my room.

"And this door stays open, do you hear me?"

"Yes, sir."

My dad walked away then, and I turned to Zach, who was pacing the length of my room like I had been just minutes earlier. I wrapped my arms around myself, holding myself together.

Then a thought hits me, *Did he have the same dream as I did just now? Is that why he's here?*

"I'm sorry to come over like this, but I really needed to talk to you," he said, still pacing.

"I went to see Mitch tonight. I just came from there actually. Sometimes I just want to kill him, you know?"

"Yeah, I know," I agreed.

"Tonight," he wrings his hands, then continues, "He tried to tell me my mom is still alive! Can you believe that guy? Then he calls The Haven, and some woman answers and starts talking about my mom as if she's still a patient there. Can you believe that? Mitch is really thorough. I can't believe he paid someone to pretend to work there."

"Wait, Mitch said what?"

This isn't about the dream?

"That my mom's still alive."

"But she died when you were a kid."

"Apparently not, or at least that's what Mitch wants me to believe. I can't believe that guy."

I just stood there, watching Zach pace. I had never seen him so upset before.

"I'm sorry, you were probably sleeping. I just had to see you." He looked up then and seemed to see me for the first time that night.

I was across the room from him, when typically I would immediately go over to him when something was wrong. Clearly, I was keeping my distance on purpose. I had enough experience to know by now that if I did go over to him and hug him or hold his hand that he would see the dream I'd had tonight. And I certainly didn't want to add to everything he was dealing with right now with a dream where I thought he'd be with my best friend.

"Ad, what's wrong? Do you think he's right?"

"What?" I shook my head and tried to focus on the present. "You know what happened, Zach. He's just trying to mess with you."

Zach finally stopped pacing and walked over to me. I took a step back.

He looked surprised at me. "Ad?"

I looked away. *You can't see this dream right now,* I thought. He reached out and gently grabbed my hand.

Then he pulled me close, wrapping me in an abrupt and tight hug. "Addison! Why didn't you say something?"

"What are you talking about?" I asked, trying to play dumb.

"That dream you had. That's horrible." He squeezed me tighter. Then he stepped back and bent his neck a bit so he could look me in the eye. "Addison, I am so sorry he put that in your head."

"It's fine," I said.

"No, it isn't fine. I can't believe he did that to you! I can't stand him," Zach said sounding angry. "Addison, I love you, okay? I would never cheat on you with Cammie. Or anyone. Ever."

"I know that. Or, at least, I thought I knew that. I don't know why my mind would even think that or go there," I said.

"You do know that," he answered, trying to reassure me. "That's him. That's not your mind. He's just trying to get to you in any way he can."

"But..." I didn't know what else I should say, or what I was trying to ask him.

"Yeah?"

"Are you looking for more? From me? Or if not from me, from other girls?"

He took a breath and told me, "Ad, we talked about all that before. You said you wanted to wait, and I'm fine with that. I love you, Ad, and I would never betray you like that. I'm sorry about that dream, but I promise that one won't come true. I won't ever go searching for other girls because everything I could ever want is right in front of me. I would wait forever for you."

I took a deep breath, trying to calm my heart rate.

"Will you come with me?" he asked quietly.

"Where?"

"To see my mom. I mean, to see if he's telling the truth. I can't go there alone in case he is." He sounded like such a little kid right then, a boy scared of the nightmares that happen in real life.

"Yeah, of course," I replied.

Then my dad knocked on my bedroom door. "Two minutes, okay, kiddos?"

"Okay, Dad," I said as he turned and walked away.

"How 'bout we go sometime this week?" Zach asked.

I nodded, and then he gently took my hands in his. "And how 'bout we change that dream if we can? You can dream of happy things like rainbows and the beach or something."

"That sounds lovely," I replied.

"You're lovely," he said, kissing my forehead as he stood to leave. "Enjoy the beach, and sweet dreams!"

He left then, and that night I did dream of the beach, all sunny and breezy, with a beautiful rainbow arching over a palm tree.

When I woke the next morning, the nightmare from the night before felt like a distant memory, replaced by sunshine and seashells and all things good. Good like Zach, the real Zach.

42

- Mitch -

Saturday, May 19th, 2018

I turn the envelope over and over in my hands. *To the Guardian of Zachary Walker* it reads in a scripted font on the front. There is the official seal for Madison High on the upper left corner.

To the Guardian of Zachary Walker.

Boy, are those six words I never thought I would see on an envelope addressed to me! I never in a million years thought I would get stuck with the kid. I still remember (and regret) the day Adam begged me to take Zach and raise him. Zach was eight, and I was only 27. I could not take care of him. I did not *want to* take care of him.

I had told Adam we would talk about it, come up with a better plan. Meg had only been in The Haven for a week. We were still doing all right; we were managing without her...barely.

But Adam, being spontaneous, carefree Adam, packed his things and was gone by the time I got home from work that day.

And in about a second (how long it took to read his "note" saying he'd left), I became Zach's guardian.

I had a whole other person to take care of when I had barely been taking care of myself.

I am about to toss the envelope in the trash. *I am no guardian,* I think. But I decide to open it, curious what it would say.

I imagine it will tell me he stopped showing up to class, he would not graduate, or he failed a class and had to go to summer school, or something of that regard.

But no.

What I see are words so shocking to me, I have to sit down.

Dear Mr. DeMize,

It is our pleasure to inform you that your student, Zachary Walker, will be graduating on Friday the twenty-fifth of May, two thousand eighteen at five o'clock in the evening.

He will be graduating with Highest Honors and as a student in the top ten percent of his graduating class. You should be very proud of his accomplishments.

Zachary has done remarkably well here at Madison High, especially being a third year transfer.

He will be receiving the *James Madison Award of Academic Excellence* as an acknowledgement of the outstanding work he has done academically at this institution.

We wanted to congratulate you and Zachary. This award is well-deserved.

Best Regards,
Principal Wilkins

Wow, I thought, *a dreamer -- a good dreamer is actually doing well in life.*

I just sit there, staring at the piece of paper that would make any parent proud. It probably would have made Meg cry.

But all I can think is how did he achieve this and I didn't.

I barely graduated. I was hanging on by a thread my whole senior year. It made me so mad some days showing up and seeing all the other kids fretting over grades and college acceptance letters when I had no chance for college. There was no way I would get it, so what was the point of even trying? I went from being the star-athlete and star-student, to the loser in the corner of the room (if he even bothered to show up), looking like he had not slept or eaten in days, because I had not.

I gave Zach the chance to have the life he has. It is all because of me.

You are welcome, I think, and toss the stupid paper in the trash.

43

- Addison -
Saturday, May 19th, 2018

"**A**re you sure you want to do this?" I asked Zach, squeezing his hand to remind him that I was there for him -- now and always. "I have to," he answered, staring straight ahead of us at the big, ominous looking gates.

We stood there for a few minutes. I watched the rise and fall of his chest as he contemplated if he really should go in.

"Yeah," he said. "I have to go now. I need to know."

"Do you want me to wait here?"

"No. Come," he replied, turning toward me.

"Okay, I will." I tried to force a reassuring smile. I wished I could have been more help. I wished I could have known what to say. *But what can you say to your boyfriend when he finds out - ten years later - that his mother might be alive after all?*

"I love you. It'll all be okay," was all I finally came up with.

"Let's go," he said and swallowed.

"All right. Let's go." I gave his hand another squeeze, and he led me up to the gates.

He pressed a button.

"Hello?" a woman's voice asked through the speaker.

I looked the building up and down. It looked like something right out of a horror film. This place would be enough to make anyone go crazy.

I almost had to laugh at the sign. "The Haven: A Safe Space For All." It was certainly no "haven" in any way, shape, or form; it looked more like a prison.

"Zach Walker," he answered when the lady asked for his name.

A buzzer sounded and the gates came to life. There was an incredibly eerie sound as they slid apart, creating an opening that would lead us to a place I really didn't want to go inside. Everything about this place, this so-called "haven", screamed at me to turn around, not to enter. It seemed like the kind of place that once you walked through the doors, you never walked back out.

We climbed the concrete steps to the cold metal front door. Zach reached out and opened it, showing us a stark white hallway with a reception desk at the end.

"Well, hello there!" the receptionist called out to us as we approached.

"Hi," Zach said sounding very somber. "I'm here to see a Meg Walker."

"You are?" the woman asked, her green eyes almost popping out of their sockets from her surprise.

"Is she a patient here?" Zach asked.

"Yes, sir. Meg's been here a long time. It's just that she doesn't get many visitors."

Zach looked deflated. I could tell he had been hoping the receptionist would've said "Meg Walker? There's no one by that name here."

This receptionist had just confirmed that Mitch was telling the truth – for once.

The receptionist spun her chair around, her curly brown hair bouncing all around, and craned her neck. "Hmm, three o'clock. She's just finishing up board game time in the main room. If you don't mind waiting five minutes, that would be great!"

This woman sounded way too chipper to have the job she does at a place like this. It annoyed me.

"Uh, sure," Zach told her.

She pointed us to three uncomfortable-looking chairs against the wall across from her desk.

Zach and I sank into them, and he let out a breath I bet he had been holding in since we arrived here.

He turned to look me in the eyes. "Thanks, Ad. I'm really glad you're here with me."

"Of course, Zach. This is the only place I'd want to be right now."

He chuckled, but it was a very sad sound. "Seriously? I'd give anything to be anywhere but here right now."

"I meant with you. I wouldn't have wanted you to have to do this alone," I clarified.

"Well, it means a lot to me – having you here, having someone to come with me."

I smiled at him. Then we sat in silence for a few minutes. I could tell he was deep in thought.

"I just," he said suddenly, breaking the silence. "How did this even happen? I thought she was dead. Clearly, she's a patient here. I mean, this place is creepy, but I doubt they keep dead people here. I've visited her grave, Ad. Who's there? Is it just an empty grave?" He stood up and stepped in front of me.

I looked up at him. "I don't know," I admitted, honestly wondering how someone could lie to their kid and say their mother died. "You were young," I suggested. "They probably told you what was easiest for them or what they thought you could handle."

"Oh please! I doubt their decision involved me at all. This is Mitch and my Dad we are talking about; they did what was best for them. Why did I fall for it though?"

"Zach, come on," I begged, trying to get him to sit down again. "You were eight. You can't blame yourself for this – any of it."

"I saw her though. She was sick. I saw it with my own eyes. She would just lie there, looking so small and so weak. I used to bring her tea each night when she asked for it. She barely spoke. She was sick. She was sick, and she died."

"Zach– "

"If you'll come this way," the too-bubbly receptionist cut in, holding a door open for us.

Zach huffed and followed her through the door; I followed a step behind.

She led us down a long corridor. It was cold and white; it reminded me of a hospital. An old, rundown hospital.

How can anyone be sane living here? I wondered.

"All right. Here we are," she said in a whisper. "Just give me one second."

She opened the door, just a crack, and angled her body to block us from view. "Nancy?" she asked, just above a whisper.

"Yes?" the nurse asked.

"I have a visitor for Mrs. Walker."

The nurse mumbled something in reply. The receptionist turned to us and smiled, "Nurse Nancy has to give Mrs. Walker her medicine first, the she'll let you in."

"Okay," Zach said. He seemed numb, unfazed by the fact his mother was on the other side of the wall. Or maybe it was just the opposite – he was numb *because* his mother was on the other side of the wall.

The receptionist turned and left us there, alone in the hallway. I heard some shouting and crying from a few rooms down the hall; it startled me, the piercing sounds in echoing in this eerie place.

A beat later Nurse Nancy, a woman in her sixties with a tired smile, opened the door and motioned for us to come in.

"Meg," she said in a soothing tone. "You have some visitors here today."

"Oh, yay!" Meg cheered, sounding about five years old. Zach's face tightened; his jaw clenched.

"I'll be right across the hall," the nurse told us. "Holler if you need me. She should be fine for a bit though."

I was about to ask what she meant by that when I saw the empty paper cup meant for pills in her hands. *What do they have her on here?*

The nurse left.

"Hello," Meg said, smiling wide.

"Hi... Mom," Zach replied.

She got the most puzzled look on her face then. I said "hello" and my name. She nodded, taking it in, but still confused by Zach's introduction.

I looked at the woman standing in front of me. She looked very tired, a little crazed, and heartbreakingly haunted. But beneath it all, she was beautiful. She had jet black hair flowing down past her shoulders with a gentle wave to it. She had a porcelain complexion, and although her eyes were a bit sunken in and sad, they were striking. She had the same unique blue that shone from Zach's familiar eyes. But thank God Zach's eyes didn't look as haunted as hers.

This woman was Zach's mom; you could see it in every piece of him. But this woman – the ghost of this woman, the absence of her – changed his life forever. I instantly felt a pang in my chest that Zach had to see her this way and that he didn't see her for such a long time.

I held my breath, as her face untwisted and realization crossed over her eyes.

"No, no, no," she whispered, shaking her head and pointing at Zach.

"What is it?" he asked, looking all around the room.

"Mrs. Walker?" I asked.

"It can't be," she mumbled.

"What can't be?" I asked, stepping a bit closer to her.

She jumped back. "Get away," she spat at us.

"I don't believe in ghosts. I don't believe in ghosts," she repeated over and over.

"Ghosts?" Zach repeated, incredulous.

"What ghosts?" I asked her in a quiet voice.

She looked me dead in the eyes, her bright blue eyes locking on mine. "My son."

"He isn't a ghost, Mrs. Walker. He came to see you," I tried.

"No, no. My baby died a long time ago. This man has his eyes though. I know it's him. It's a ghost; it's a ghost!" she accused, still in a hushed tone. I could tell she wanted to scream, but maybe she didn't want to draw attention.

"Mom, it's me. Zachary. I'm sorry I didn't come sooner." Zach looked like he could cry.

What is going on here? I wondered. *What does she mean 'my baby died a long time ago'?*

I took a step closer to Zach and took his hand in mine again. "It's okay," I whispered. "Maybe we should come back later."

"Mom?" he asked again.

"Stop it!" she yelled. "My son is dead."

"No, Mom, I'm here."

Nurse Nancy came in then. "It's time for Meg's nap. I think she needs some rest." "Wait," Zach stopped her. "I have to talk to her."

"That's enough for today. Visiting hours are over. I suggest you come back later."

"But – "

"Zach, it's okay. We'll come back later."

The nurse was helping Meg lie down on the mattress. She looked back up at us as I tried to usher Zach out of the room.

"Who did you say you were?" she asked in a suspicious tone.

"I'm her son," Zach said.

"Oh, Meg, I didn't know you had two sons. That's nice your boy came to visit you," the nurse said patting Meg's arm.

As she came to the door, I stuttered, "Two sons? Why did you say you didn't know she had two sons?"

"Meg's son died shortly after she was admitted here. He's all she talks about. Sounded like a sweet boy. I'm sorry," she said turning to Zach. "I never realized she had another boy."

"She didn't," Zach mumbled and turned. He walked down the long hallway and straight out the door.

"Zach, wait!" I called after him. *What just happened?*

I ran out the doors after him. He stopped suddenly, right before the big gates, and I slammed into his back.

"Zach," I started. "Are you okay?"

He turned around to face me. He reached out, gripping my shoulders and forcing me to look him in the eye. "She's alive," he said with a glimmer in his blue eyes that were so much like hers.

"She's alive, Addison," he repeated, shaking my shoulders to emphasize his point. "She's alive... and I'm going to do everything I can to help her get out of there."

I took a step closer and wrapped my arms around him.

"She's alive," he echoed, over and over.

Graduation Day

44

- Addison -
Friday, May 25th, 2018

"**A**ddison Grace Smith," the principal called out.

I stood. I looked back at my mom, eyes red with tears, sitting in between my father who was smiling proudly and my aunt who was looking almost sad.

I smiled at them, took a breath, and walked across the stage, accepting the diploma that most dreamers like me never get.

I had made it. I finished high school. I could go out now and do what I wanted, be what I wanted. I already had an important piece of paper that was my golden ticket out of Madison, out of this crazy town of dreamers and memories.

I was leaving in a week on a journey that would change my life and *heal* my mind.

It's crazy sometimes how moments you spend so much time wondering about, working toward, and obsessing over and over go by very quickly. It's like Christmas: you shop, wrap the presents, decorate the house, listen to Christmas carols every day from

Thanksgiving on, and then in a mere twenty-four hours it's over. Or a wedding: people spend months and months planning, waiting anxiously for the day, and then there's a rush of people and "Congratulations!" and then the wedding is over in a couple of hours. Today is like that. You spend your entire academic career up until this point studying, taking tests, writing papers, counting down the days until summer vacation, and then one day you start counting down the days until graduation. It seems like the day will never come. You order your cap and gown, apply to colleges, continue to study, and then suddenly the day is here. And in the movies, there's always this long graceful walk across a stage to receive your diploma, but in reality, it's a pretty short walk, and then it takes two seconds for the principal to hand you the diploma, and that's it. You've graduated. You're done. You work year after year for something that is done in about two seconds.

Sometimes I wish dreaming could be that way, over in a second. I wish it were that easy to get Mitch out of my head and change my dreams.

Just then, walking back to my alphabetically assigned seat, I saw him standing in the back of the gym.

My mind flashed to the dream of homecoming I had during the coma, where I was standing in this same gym, all decorated and dark for the school dance, when suddenly I saw him across the room, standing where he was standing right now.

I must have been dreaming.

There's no way Mitch would come to graduation.

Zach didn't even tell him when it was. And even if he had told Mitch when it was, Mitch wasn't the type of uncle to come and support and congratulate his nephew.

So why was he here?

He saw me looking at him and grinned. He nodded his head in a gesture that would appear to mean "congratulations," but I knew better. I'm sure it meant something more like "game on."

I almost tripped over one of the folding chairs while navigating over the gowns, the other students' legs, and the row of chairs on the other side of me. So, to avoid falling on my face in front of the entire school and everyone's families, I turned my gaze away from Zach's uncle and concentrated on getting back to my seat in one piece.

"Rebecca Elliott Vall," the principal called out.

I knew what was coming next, and my heart swelled with happiness for him.

Principal Wilkins leaned close to the microphone and read, "Zachary David Walker."

I clapped along with the crowd for him.

Sometimes I just looked at him and wondered how I got so lucky. I mean, it all started with a dream. I quite literally ran into him one day, and look where we are now.

After Zach sat down, winking at me on his way back to his seat, the kids at the end of the alphabet were called and received their diplomas.

Then the valedictorian, a very sweet girl I had a couple classes with over the years named Emilee, gave her speech. It was about our futures, how we all have the rest of our lives to become exactly who we are meant to be. She said today is the start of our futures, the beginning of a dream come true; we just have to go out there and follow our dreams.

Little did she, or any of my other classmates, know that I was in fact following my dreams soon. And I intend to follow my dreams and overcome my nightmares.

Then the guidance counselor stepped up to the podium. "Next, I will be presenting the James Madison Award of Academic Excellence. This award is given to one graduating senior who has shown tremendous effort in their studies. Each teacher nominates a deserving student to receive this award. This year, the results were almost unanimous."

I looked around the room, all the people sitting upright in anticipation, parents pulling out their phones to capture the moment should their child's name be called. I'm sure it'll be given to the valedictorian or salutatorian.

"This year this award goes to Mr. Zachary Walker," she announced, and I just about died.

I twisted in my chair, trying to find him. He was just sitting there, looking confused. Then he composed himself, and his signature, charming smile appeared on his face as he walked up to the front to get the award. As he walked up, I noticed he had an extra set of cords around his neck.

Zach got highest honors?

My boyfriend, a dreamer, who never thought he'd even graduate high school because of his family history of flunking out due to dreams. And yet here he was, graduating, and not only graduating, but doing so with highest honors. I was barely holding my grades together, and I knew he got less sleep than I did; I didn't know how he did it, but he did it.

"Yes, Walker!" Jake called out as Zach shook the counselor's hand.

"Congratulations, Zachary," the guidance counselor said.

I pulled my eyes away from Zach just long enough to turn back to where Mitch still stood and give him the worst look I've probably ever given anyone. With one look I said: "you should be so proud of him -- you tried to hold him back -- but look at him now -- you will never be half the person he is -- and he is already a hundred times the man you are. You don't deserve to be in his life -- and I'm glad you were here to see this moment - to see how great your nephew has done in this screwed up world." Yes, I tried to say all of that in a single glance. And based on the shocked expression on Mitch's face right before I turned back toward the stage, he got it.

* * *

Later that night we sat around a bonfire roasting marshmallows and telling stories and memories from the past four years. I sat between Zach and Cammie, the best parts of high school.

I looked up and stared into the orange flames for a minute, losing my thoughts to the fire. My eyes focused on the person on the other side of the fire. As the flames flickered up in front of her face, she smiled at me and I smiled at her, happy to call Jess my friend again.

Cammie curled up and tucked her head into my neck, "I'm going to miss you so much, Addie!"

"I'm not leaving yet," I told her.

"I know, but I'm still going to miss you."

"I'll miss you, too, but we'll stay in touch. I promise," I vowed.

"I know we will, but it'll be different. We go from seeing each other every single day, -- really, multiple times a day, to only on breaks?"

"Cammie," I started, wishing we hadn't just started this conversation because I knew it would end with someone crying.

"I know, I know," she said, running a finger under her eye to catch a tear. "There goes my makeup! I'll be right back." She jumped up and made her way through the other kids, going into the house.

I sighed.

Zach tightened his arm around me. "Hey, pretty girl," he said.

"Hey, my super-smart, incredible guy," I said.

"Can we talk?"

"Uh, sure," I told him, and stood up, placing the blanket Cam and I had been sharing on the seat, and followed Zach to the edge of the woods, close enough to the group but far enough we were alone and out of earshot.

"So, listen," he started and took my hand.

"Yeah?"

"Obviously, I don't want you to leave for the whole summer, but I know this is something you have to do, and I want things to get better for you, so you have to go."

"Aw, Zach, I'm going to miss you, too," I told him, and squeezed his hand in mine.

"I need to know you're going to be okay," he said quieter.

"I will be."

"No, Ad, I need you to promise me you'll be careful. Don't go dreaming yourself to any strange places, and don't try any vudu magic stuff. And whatever you do, don't even think about Mitch, don't even let him in your head, okay? Try to block him from your mind, and while I'm over here, I'll try to make it harder for him to find your brainwaves even if he wanted to."

"Okay, I promise," I told him.

"Okay, good. Because I need you to come back here the same awesome you that you are. Just less nightmares."

"I love you," I whispered. "I'm going to figure this out, and Jess will be there, so we can help each other and protect each other. I want to find a cure for this, like Carrie did. I'm going to go and find a way for me and Jess and you and any other dreamers to have a normal life. But I'm not going to let myself forget the best dream I've ever had ... you."

Zach looked up, then suddenly turned me around and pointed up at the night sky. "Quick! Make a wish!" he instructed as a little white light flashed across the sky.

RODGERS

I closed my eyes and wished that everything would work out, and that dreams or no dreams, I would always have a reason to feel as happy as I did right then.

One Week Later...

45

- Addison -
Friday, June 1ˢᵗ, 2018

$\mathcal{T}$he sound of a piano woke me from a surprisingly pleasant dream.
That sound was followed by the sound of a rooster. Then finally the
sound of a siren blaring.

"If you don't turn that off, I will throw that phone at you!"

I rolled over and turned off all three of the alarms I had set on
my phone to make sure I did not oversleep today.

"Sorry, Jess! I just didn't want to sleep through my alarm," I
explained in a whisper.

"The whole neighborhood couldn't have slept through all the
alarms you set today!" she yelled at me.

"Someone's not a morning person," I grumbled, getting out of
bed.

"I am! But I am not a three-o'clock-in-the-morning person!"
She turned over in her sleeping bag so she was facing away from me.

"Jess, get up. We can't miss our flight."

"No," she mumbled.

"Jess, come on," I begged, while I double, then triple, checked that everything in my carry-on was together; phone charger, outlet converter, my lucky bracelet I always wear on planes, a book, a brand-new journal, headphones, and snacks for the plane ride.

"Jess," I called out again.

"Just five more minutes."

I picked up a fuzzy black pillow from my bed and chucked it at her.

"Hey!" she yelled. But she got up in an instant.

"Do you have everything?" I asked her.

"Addison, do you realize you asked me that thirteen times last night?"

"Sorry! I'm excited. And nervous."

"I couldn't tell," she said with a smirk.

"So, do you have everything?"

"Yes!" she answered, and crawled over to my desk and picked something up. When she turned back around I gasped.

"What?" she snapped.

"You wear glasses?"

"Yes, didn't you know that?"

"No."

She had these dorky-looking bug-eyed glasses that made her eyes look huge. I don't think I had ever seen her with glasses before. Like ever. I think I had just always assumed little miss perfect had twenty-twenty vision.

She zipped up all her bags, then looked at me and warned, "If you ask me one more time if I have everything, I'm not coming on this trip."

"Okay, okay! Sorry."

"So why isn't your aunt coming?" she asked, brushing out her now-short hair.

"I don't really know," I admitted, as I changed out of my pajama shorts into my jeans. "I think it's too hard for her sometimes. It's like she's blocked out part of her life. She helped a lot planning the trip, but every time I'd ask her to come with us, she would say she couldn't and then just shut down."

"I think it would've been helpful if she came," Jess said.

"I know, me too. But --"

"Good morning, girlies! Are you guys ready to go on our journey?" my mom exclaimed and walked into my room.

"First stop, Paris!" I sang.

An hour later we pulled up by the curb at the airport. My dad got our bags from the trunk and hugged me tight. "Have a wonderful time, sweetheart! I'm so proud of you," he said and kissed my forehead.

My parents said goodbye as I turned around looking up and down the curb side. "Where's Aunt Carrie?" I asked. I had thought she was meeting us here to say goodbye before she went to work.

"She couldn't make it," my mom explained. I could hear the disappointment in her voice.

"Oh," I said, unzipping my purse to make sure, for the seventh time, that I had my passport.

"All right, well, we better get rolling!" my mom said, hugging my dad again.

"Let me know when you land," he told her.

"Of course." She nodded and took her luggage from him.

Then we walked through the automatic double doors into the big airport and set off on our trip. I was almost shaking with excitement and nerves.

The plan was to fly into Paris where we would stay for a few days because -- well, we were *in Paris*! Then we would take another plane from Paris to southern France where I've heard miracles happen. Then from there, we head to Ireland to a place known for healing of the soul and mind. We would end the European part of the trip in Italy, at a place that my research says will heal your mind and heart. From there, we would travel to the sites my aunt saw in India.

Hours later, high above the clouds, I watched the screen on the back of the seat in front of me. The little tiny airplane symbol was slowly moving across the screen as we were slowly moving across the Atlantic Ocean. Jess was to my left sleeping soundly. Mom was to my right paging through a home decorating magazine.

She saw me looking and smiled, "What's up, buttercup?"

I decided to ask her the question I had been asking myself for the past few weeks. "Mom," I started, turning toward her in my seat. "Am I doing the right thing?"

"What do you mean? The trip?"

"Yeah. The trip, everything. What if I'm not really supposed to go? What if none of this helps me? What if I'm just crazy and no amount of miraculous water can save me from myself? What if I just wasted our money and our time coming over here on some wild goose chase that's a dead end? What if --"

"Honey," she interrupted, with a small smile on her face. "I love you. You are not crazy, okay? You are not wasting a second of my time, ever. You are worth every moment, and I would fly to any country I could if it meant giving you peace of mind. I'm sure one of these places will help you. But remember, Addison, everything in life happens for a reason."

"I know, Mom. But what is the reason for this?" I asked.

"You may never know the reason, my darling daughter. That's where faith comes in. You just have to believe that this journey will heal you, and it will if that's what's meant to happen. Maybe you're meant to do this because you just need a break from your normal life, to get away and breathe. Maybe there is no purpose for this trip other than to give you wonderful memories to replace the old ones with. Maybe you're meant to get closer with Jess. Maybe you're meant to learn more about yourself and find out who you are meant to be in this life. Or maybe, just maybe, if you believe deeply enough, this journey will heal your mind, your soul, and your body -- because you are a beautiful, wonderful girl, and you deserve the best that life has to offer. And I hope this trip helps you find that."

I took a breath and took that all in. *She's right,* I thought, as much as I hated to admit it, *I might never know why I decided to go to the places I chose. But I'll never know until I go.*

"You're right, Mom. Thank you," I told her and leaned my head on her shoulder. "I love you, Mom."

"I love you, too, baby girl," she replied, smoothing my hair back.

* * *

Much later that night after landing in Paris and roaming the streets of the city, we saw a bright light peeking out between two buildings.

"OH, MY GOSH! There it is!" Jess squealed, pointing.

We walked down the stone street, two old cream-colored buildings with black awnings and wrought iron balconies rising up on both sides of us. It was beautiful and incredible, like the brightest, most beautiful light at the end of a tunnel, far at first, but quickly appearing nearer and brighter in the fading sky.

Then it was in front of us. The Eiffel Tower, twinkling and lighting up the sky like nothing I have ever seen, in real life or in my dreams. I was faintly aware of my mother looking at the tower in awe and snapping pictures on our camera and Jess turning around to take a picture of her face in front of the glowing structure. But I just stood still and stared. I couldn't believe where I was standing, what I was seeing. It was incredibly beautiful. It was breathtaking. It was like a dream, the very best kind.

46

- Mitch -

Friday, June 1st, 2018

I decide to go see my sister this afternoon. I do actually go to see her quite often, despite what people may think of me. She is my sister, after all. I would not just abandon her at a place like The Haven. I saw what they did to my mother after all.

But Meg was sick… not physically like we told Zach back then. She was sick mentally, like she always was. Like I am. Like all dreamers are. She needed help. It really was the only way.

However, Meg was nothing if not stubborn. She sure did put up a fight. She would never leave Zachary.

I must say Adam is quite a guy - and I mean this in the most sarcastic way possible. He is a jerk. You know that saying that girls always find a guy with qualities like their father? Meg did just that.

Adam has always reminded me of my father. He is impatient and judgemental and at the first sign of trouble he flees. He is a wimp.

The man left his eight-year-old with someone like me. What does that say about his character and judgement?

Adam comes to me one day with this grand plan. It was just crazy enough to work, though. Within a week he had Meg admitted, signed the papers to make me Zach's guardian, and rented an apartment across the country and moved there.

He had impeccable timing, though. Meg had been pretty out of it for days, drained from the many nightmares. She had not left the house in a while, and when she did leave, everyone could visibly see she was sick. Now, this was all an effect of her dreams, but Adam used this to make his story more believable. When he said Meg had passed away, of course everyone who knew Meg and had seen her within the last few months would not question a thing. They all gave their condolences, sent flowers, and brought casseroles to the house. I watched as Adam put on this grand show, pretending to be a caring, guilt-ridden husband.

He was weak. He saw things getting out of control with Meg. But rather than trying to help her through it all - through sickness and health as he had promised her years before - he bolted and abandoned his son.

I am still unsure what exactly he told Meg after she was admitted to The Haven. She has never been able to bring herself to tell me what Adam said happened. All she knows, all she believes, is that her son - the only thing that ever gave her the will to live, to keep pushing forward in this crappy thing called life - had died in some tragic accident.

The nurses there affirmed this time and time again. I tried early on to tell her the truth. But she was so full of grief, she could not even hold it together after hearing Zach's name.

But now...

I walk into her room, wearing my visitor's badge. "Hi, Meg," I say with a smile.

I stop dead in my tracks in the doorway.

"Zach?" I ask, looking at my nephew sitting beside his mother in her issued slippers and robe.

"Hi," he nods.

"So, you came to see if I was telling the truth after all?" I inquire, still surprised he is here.

"Actually, I came before graduation. I've been visiting since then," Zach tells me.

"Mitch!" Meg cuts in.

"Hello," I greet her again.

She jumps up from the bed and rushes over to me. "Mitch! Look at my boy, look how grown up he is! He's here to see me!"

"I can see that," I tell her, eyeing her son.

"I never thought this could happen!" she squeals.

I do not think I have seen Meg so excited since the day she brought Zach home from the hospital. She had stopped by my apartment on their way home, wanting me to come to their new mini-van and see Zach sleeping soundly in their new car seat. "Look how perfect he is! Look at him sleeping! I bet he's dreaming!" she had exclaimed to me.

She runs back over to Zach now, squeezing him in a tight bear hug.

Then she whirls on me, looking furious. "You lied to me," she accuses.

"Meg -" I start.

"No! You're a liar! You! You said my son was dead. You all said that."

"Meg, you wouldn't have stayed here if you -"

"Get out!" she screams.

"Mom," Zach reaches out and lightly touches Meg's shoulder.

Then suddenly she spins on him. "You're a ghost! My son is dead. Get out! Who are you?"

Zach looks at me scared.

"Meg, this is Zach. He's your son," I try.

"No, no, no, no, no," she repeats, gripping her hair and pulling at it.

"Zach, go get Nancy," I order him. I can tell she is slipping away again, back into the dark places of her mind. He really should not see this.

"But, I want to help."

"Zachary, now. Go!"

He runs out of the room, calling for a nurse.

"It's okay, Meg. It'll be okay," I say, taking her in my arms like I have so many times growing up. I always feel like I am the older sibling in times like this. Sometimes it feels like she's ten-years-old and screaming for our parents.

Nancy, Meg's main nurse, comes in then and injects something into Meg's arm that instantly makes her eyes go blank.

I walk outside and see Zach leaning against the wall. "What happened in there? It was like she flipped a switch or something," he asks. He looks eight-years-old again.

"It happens, sometimes."

"I don't think they're helping her here, Mitch," he whispers. "I don't. We need to get her out."

"No one ever leaves The Haven, my boy," I say, surprised at myself for the sadness coating my voice.

"That can't be true," he counters.

"Oh, but it is."

"Why do you even come?" he asks.

I am taken aback by his bluntness and annoyed tone. "She's my sister," I say.

"She's your sister?" he laughs. "You're kidding, right? If you really cared that much about her you would have helped her! You would have gotten her out of here! You would have TOLD ME SHE WAS ALIVE!" He is yelling now. I do not care though; the nurses can look and gossip all they want.

"You don't understand the situation."

"No, I'm pretty sure I understand, *Uncle*. You told your kid nephew his mother died so there would be no questions asked. You told your sister her son died so there would be no fight when you tried to bring her here. I know she would've gotten better, would've gotten out of this place if she knew."

"Exactly," I say. "She never would have stayed and gotten the help she did."

"The help?" Zach yells. "Did you see her just now? She's gone completely insane!"

"Zach, calm down," I try, now worried his yelling will stir up all the other patients.

He stands up straight and stalks down the hall and out of the building.

I follow him.

"You don't care about her! You don't care about anyone but yourself," he calls over his shoulder.

"That is not true, Zachary. That is far from true. Everything I have done has been to help Meg, to make up for what happened to my mom, your grandmother."

"Torturing Addison? That was to help my mom? How, Mitch?" he accuses, turning on me.

"Now you listen to me," I tell him, pointing my index finger at him. "I raised you. I taught you everything I know. You turned on me. You threw all of our plans away for some girl."

"She's not just some girl, Mitch. And you know that."

"No, she's not. She better be careful or I won't be her only concern. They'll find her and they'll be after her next," I respond.

"I'm not going to let anything happen to her," he says in a way that's pointed at me.

I decide to ask him the question I have asked myself a few times recently. "Where are you living?"

He looks surprised I have asked this. "With a friend," he says, scuffing his shoe on the ground.

"With a friend? For close to two years?" I challenge.

"Well, I was staying back at your apartment, our apartment… until you moved back," he says.

I nod. *Figures. The school had me listed as his guardian, so he could be living there on his own no questions asked because I am sure they assumed I was living there as well.*

"Well, there's no way you can stay with this friend all summer," I point out.

Mitch, what are you doing? I warn myself.

"So? What do you care?" he spits out.

"Why don't you move back in?"

"What?" he asks, incredulous.

"I'm going away for a bit. I'm going off to find some old friends of mine. I need to get back on track. You can stay there while I am gone. It is only a few miles from here, so you can visit her if you choose to," I explain.

"I…uh…thanks, Uncle Mitch," he says, no sarcasm in the way he calls me "Uncle."

"Sure, kid," I say.

I pat him on the back and walk down the pathway, through the gates, and get in my car.

Then I drive and drive until I reach another small town, not too far from and almost exactly like Madison.

I sit in their town square, at a café, as the bell tower rings out that it is four o'clock in the afternoon.

"Hello, Mitchell. Good to see you," a raspy voice says, as the woman sits in the chair across from me.

I take a slow sip of my coffee. "Hello."

"So, I take it you want my help now?" she asks.

"Yes," I tell the woman I have not seen in at least ten years. I met her during my studies and search for answers.

"Alright, so…" she starts, looking around to make sure no one can hear. "I have a plan. We are finally going to stop *them*."

"I'm in," I say, and she grins.

"Well, then, I am very glad that you called."

47

- Addison -
Saturday, June 2ⁿᵈ, 2018

I'm running in an open field full of wildflowers. They are yellow, bright and shining in the sunlight. I can feel their soft petals against my legs as I run through the field.

Someone's chasing me.

I can feel it.

It's Mitch. It has to be. *Why can't he just leave me alone?*

Suddenly, the sunshine fades away. Big grey clouds tumble in above me, darkening everything in view. Thunder rumbles. The wind howls and blows some of the bright petals off the flowers. I watch as they float in the wind, far, far away.

The petals that don't fly away darken. No longer a bright, cheery yellow, but instead a dull, dead brown color. They crumble and wither to the ground as I run.

It's an endless field. It just goes on and on with nothing but these dead wildflowers in sight.

Lightning strikes down in front of me, so close I jump back and then fall to the ground, surrounded by the dead flowers and dead grass.

Just change it, I think to myself as the electric, purple flash shoots back up into the sky where it came from. *Change the dream.*

But it isn't working this time; nothing is changing.

Then comes the rain.

A torrential downpour all around me, but not touching me. It's almost like I'm in a bubble, a bubble where the storm can't get to me.

Thunder roars from the clouds, and lightning strikes. Wind is stirring up all of the leaves and flowers, and it sounds like screams as it blows.

My personal little bubble is growing, expanding. It's like a shield.

Pop!

Then there's water rushing all over me, and soon it feels like I am in an ocean with waves crashing over me.

Help! I call out to anyone and no one at the same time. I know this is a dream. I know I am alone. I know no one can help me now.

"Wake up, Addison," a voice calmly instructs me.

"Jess?" I ask and take a quick breath before another wave slams into my face, filling my mouth with seawater.

"Wake up, Addison," she says again.

"I don't know how!"

"Yes, you do. Just wake up."

As if it's that simple, I think.

"It is that simple, Addie. Wake up," she responds.

How did she hear me? Did I say that out loud? I wonder. But then I remember that this is the dream realm; anything can happen here.

"Hello, Addison," Mitch's eerie voice says, too close for comfort.

"Get out of my head!" I yell at him.

"You can't get rid of me, Addison," he warns.

"Yes, Addison, you can," Jess says, but I can't see her now. "Wake up. Hurry!"

Please, God, I think, *let me wake up.*

I close my eyes, and I picture where I really am, the tiny hotel room a few blocks away from the Eiffel Tower with its red damask bedding and gold floral drapes.

Then, a breath later, I woke up, lying in the bed with the red bedding next to the window with the golden drapes. *I did it,* I thought. *I woke myself up.*

Then I stood and walked over to the window. I eased back the side of the drapes, letting some of the lights from the Paris nightlife wash in through the window.

"Told you that you could do it," Jess said, barely above a whisper, but enough to startle me.

"What?"

"The dream. I knew you could get yourself out of it."

"How?" I asked her.

"Because you don't even realize how powerful you are. That would have taken me months of training, but you just willed yourself out of a dream. You're powerful, Addison, and you don't even realize it," she told me before pulling a blanket tighter over herself and falling back to sleep.

I turned and looked out the window. Everyone always told me how "powerful" I was. But I didn't feel very powerful. I wasn't some super-dreamer; I was just Addison.

I pulled out my journal and wrote about everything we had seen in Paris, from the Louvre to Notre Dame to the streets full of bakeries and shops. I wrote about this young girl we met outside of Notre Dame. We were standing on one of the side streets listening to a man play the accordion -- it sounded lovely! Then this young girl walked by and Jess stopped her, asking in French if she wouldn't mind taking our picture. My mom handed the girl our camera, and the girl took our picture.

After she took the photo, she handed my mom back the camera and turned to me, flashed a smile, her bright eyes shining. "Merci!" I told her. She walked up closer to me, took my hand and spoke so quickly I couldn't catch much of it. Then she turned and started talking to Jess in rapid French. Jess had no trouble keeping up in the conversation.

A bit later, the accordion man's song ended and he began another one, people crowding around to listen. The girl said goodbye to us all and then walked away.

"What did she say?" I asked Jess.

"She lives down that street over there with her family. She's lived here almost her whole life. She told me a little cafe we should try for dinner. She asked if we were sisters. She told me about Notre Dame and said she liked your name."

"She said all that?" I asked, shocked because they hadn't been talking all that long. "What was her name?"

"She said it was Honoré."

My mom clapped as the man's second song ended. "I love all of the music!" she exclaimed.

I looked at Jess. "Hey, did you catch what she said to me?"

"Yeah, well, kind of. I'm pretty sure she said, 'Never let your nightmares stop you from chasing your dreams.'"

"What? That seems like a strange thing to say."

"Not really, considering she's a dreamer, too."

"What? How could you tell?"

"You couldn't?" Jess asked incredulous. "You should really start paying attention to people's eyes," she said. "They tell a lot about a person."

"So she knew I'm a dreamer?" I asked Jess.

"Probably."

"Wow." I guess I never thought of other dreamers outside of Madison Town. I also never realized just how much I have to learn from Jessica Clark.

I thought about what that girl had said as I looked down at my journal. I scribbled her words down on the page:

"Never let your nightmares stop you from chasing your dreams."

From now on, I won't. I promise.

Then I closed my journal and went back to sleep, willing myself to have good dreams only, not to even let Mitch into my mind.

And for once, it worked.

48

- Addison -
Sunday, June 3rd, 2018

The next day we went back to Notre Dame because it was just so beautiful. When we walked into the church, I was blown away by how beautiful it was inside. There was a circular stained-glass window up high on the wall to my left. I watched the sunlight pour through the window and make the colors seem to dance in the air around me. The architecture was incredible; the whole place just felt beautiful and... holy.

"Oh! Look at this, Mrs. Smith!" Jess exclaimed, pulling my mom over to look at a statue of Mary.

"Hello."

I turned, startled, but also surprised the woman was speaking English.

"Hi," I said quietly.

"Isn't that incredible?" she asked, pointing to a display on the wall.

"Oh, yes, it is," I replied, taking in her cheery smile and her black and white habit.

"Do you know what this is?" she asked.

I was a little confused why she was talking to me, almost as if she knew me, but I didn't know who she was.

"Uh, no, I don't," I replied, forcing a smile, trying to be polite.

"Well, they say an image of the Virgin Mary was seen in the smoke coming from the train. That's what this is depicting," she explained in a reverent tone. "It was quite a miracle."

"I could use a miracle."

A second after the words left my mouth I regretted saying them out loud and was ashamed for being so rude to this nice nun who was trying to talk to me.

"Well, sometimes miracles come in unexpected places."

I nodded and smiled at her, then turned my head, just a little, to see where my mom and Jess had gone off to. They were right behind me, looking at another statue.

"Why are you here?" she asked, a little abruptly.

"I'm sorry?"

"What brings you here? To France? To Notre Dame? To this depiction of the train?"

"Uh, I'm not sure. I'm just looking for some answers and some healing."

"Well, my dear, if you're looking for healing, you've come to the right place."

"I have?"

"Yes. Notre Dame is dedicated to the Blessed Mother. But I think I know where you can find the healing you're looking for," she said.

"Where?" I asked. *Honestly, I would go anywhere if it meant I could find the answers Carrie found.*

She leaned close and whispered to me, "Lourdes. It is home to many miracles, all from the intercession of Our Lady. You're going there, aren't you?"

I recognized the name of the town in southern France where we were headed soon and nodded.

"Lourdes is where miracles happen and dreams come true," she said with a wink.

Did she just say dreams? Can she tell I'm a dreamer, too?

"What did you say?" I asked.

"Follow your dreams to Lourdes, my dear. Your miracle is waiting for you there. Dreams do come true, Addison."

"Thank you," I replied.

She turned to leave, and I realized then that I hadn't told her my name.

"Excuse me," I called after her.

She stopped and turned back to face me. "Yes, dear?"

"Do I know you?" I asked.

"Maybe. But I know you," she said, and for some reason I felt very calm. I wasn't at all freaked out that this woman I had never met seemed to know so much about me.

"What's your name?" I asked her, thinking maybe that would jog my memory. *Maybe I had met her before.*

"Sister Margaret-Mary," she answered, smiled, and walked away.

"Who was that?" Jess asked, walking up. "It looked like she knew you."

"Sister Margaret-Mary."

"Ok. Do you know Sister Margaret-Mary?"

"I'm not sure. But she said I should go to this place called Lourdes, that my miracle is waiting there."

"Lourdes? Isn't that the place we are going tomorrow?"

"Yeah, that's the place," I answered, still staring ahead, watching the nun walk up a row of pews and out of the church.

"Well, isn't that incredible," Mom said, staring up at the depiction of the vision of Mary in the clouds of the train.

"Yeah," I agreed. "It was quite a miracle."

My miracle is waiting for me in Lourdes, the nun had said.

I really hoped she was right.

Epilogue
- Addison -
Monday, June 4th, 2018

*W*e stepped off the little jumper plane we took from Paris to this town called Lourdes where, according to Sister Margaret-Mary, miracles happen and dreams come true.

The sun was shining through the clouds looking almost magical.

"I feel like a celebrity!" Jess squealed as she put on her big black shades and dramatically walked down the steps of the plane onto the tarmac. "It's like our own private jet!"

I turned to look back at the plane behind us, which by the way was not at all as glamorous as a private jet, but it got us where we had to go and made Jess feel like a princess, so I guess it was pretty cool.

In the tiny little airport, after getting our bags, my mom was dialling a number on her phone to call for a car to come pick us up and bring us to the hotel. Jess and I looked around their little gift shop.

There were religious items, bags, t-shirts that said "I love Lourdes!", and magazines in French. I looked through a display of postcards and found one with a picture of the Pyrenees mountains, which run along the border of France and Spain. "Wish you were here!" it read in big bubble letters along the mountaintops.

I walked over to the cashier and handed him a euro for the postcard.

"Is that for someone special?" Jess asked in a teasing voice.

"Maybe," I said, tucking the postcard away in my purse to send to Zach later.

"The car is here!" my mom called to us. We walked out the door and gave our bags to the driver, and once he put them in the trunk of the little black car, we were off, driving down winding, rural roads.

In the front of the car, the driver was chatting with my mom about the history of the town, pointing out farms and houses as we drove past them.

Jess rested her head against the window, looking like she was ready for a nap, and I turned to look out the window and watch as we drove past fields, old brick farmhouses, and sheep, lots of sheep.

"Well, here you are," the driver said a little while later, putting the car in park in front of a blue hotel that sat across from a river.

"Merci," my mother thanked him and paid the fare.

"I need a nap!" Jess complained, as we walked in the double doors of the hotel.

"Okay, let's all take a nap, and then we will go exploring," Mom suggested.

* * *

Later that afternoon, well-rested and with full stomachs, the three of us grabbed our sweaters because it was a little chilly outside and walked down to the concierge desk. We grabbed pamphlets and maps of the area and were looking through them.

"There's a service in a half hour," the concierge said in broken English.

"A service?" my mom asked.

"Yes, down by the grotto." The lady pulled out a map and drew a circle in red pen. Then she drew a line in red from the hotel to the circle. "About a fifteen-minute walk," she explained. "The service is absolutely beautiful. A must-see!"

"What kind of service is it?" Jess asked.

"Mass," the lady said, nodding her head. "It is outside; very beautiful."

"Why not?" my mom said, and we walked out the double doors and headed in the direction of the red circle she drew on the map.

We walked down cobblestone streets, past a little farmers' market and cafes. Jess and my mom kept stopping to look in the windows of the little shops at the shoes and purses.

"Come on," I begged them, "I don't want to miss the service. It sounds really nice."

"Okay, okay, we will come back later though!" my mom said, still staring back at the ballet flats in the display.

We walked past little tables people had set up along the streets selling little statues, rosaries, and prayer cards. "Holy water! Holy water!" a man called as we walked by.

When we got to where the circle was drawn on the map, we walked through a gate and down a steep hill.

"What is this place?" Jess asked.

"Lourdes," I answered, knowing this was the heart of the town. This place was special; I could feel it.

"Yeah, I know the town is called Lourdes, but where are we right now..." she trailed off when she saw what I saw.

We came up to a huge church; a beautiful church with a tower that reached up high into the sky; the church seemed to almost be reaching the clouds. There was a crown of gold at the center with a big cross coming up from the center of the crown.

"It's beautiful," my mom gasped.

"It's incredible," Jess said in awe of the amazing structure.

"It's my miracle," I said so quietly I knew no one heard me.

Do you ever just get a feeling like you are exactly where you need to be? Well, I felt that way right then. Deep within me, I knew that nun was right. My miracle was waiting here for me.

Just then, I heard a voice, a voice I would recognize anywhere, call out from behind me. "Hi, sweet pea! Oh, I've missed my little buddy!" she sang.

I spun around.

"Aunt Carrie?" I asked incredulously. I turned to Jess, "Am I dreaming?" I asked.

"I'm not sure," Jess said, sounding shocked herself.

"What are you doing here?" I asked my aunt, trying to figure out what she would be doing here when she seemed so against coming with us.

"Just thought I'd stop and see my favorite niece!" she exclaimed as she wrapped me in a hug and held me tight.

"In France?" I asked.

"Carrie, what are you doing here?" Mom asked. "I thought you--"

My aunt cut her off, saying, "Had nowhere else more important to be than with my niece on her journey."

I just stared at her. I couldn't believe my eyes.

"Well, let's go, girlies! We don't want to miss the service. I hear it's beautiful!" Carrie squealed, linking arms with my mom and beginning to walk further down the hill to where the service was held by the river.

Aunt Carrie really came to help me! I thought to myself, watching her walk with her sister, smiling so brightly and seeming so happy.

Sister Margaret-Mary had been right after all. My miracle was waiting for me in Lourdes. I could feel it deep within me. It was like my whole life was leading me to this point.

I may not have known the exact reason why I was there; I hoped that it was to end my living nightmare. But I did know it was where I was meant to be. It was like I could hear this place calling my name, like a mantra, like an echo, drawing me here so I could be healed.

I never could have dreamed of Aunt Carrie showing up here. I just didn't think she would come. But she did, and that is even more proof to me that this journey was meant to happen and that everything will work out.

I took a breath, and I took a seat. I felt a sense of calm, almost as if the healing process had already begun.

Then I folded my hands and said a quiet prayer asking for healing and for grace and for sweet dreams and a happily ever after.

And sitting there, under the shining sun, I could feel it in my bones, that for once, I might get just that. All my dreams just might come true.

Please let this work. Please, I begged.

End of Book Two

Acknowledgements:

Thank you a million times over to my readers for wanting to know the rest of Addison's story and sticking with me through this series. You were my motivation to continue writing this story!

Thank you to my beta readers: Maria, Matthew, Lisa, Wendy, Emily, Nino, and Holly, for all your insight and excitement surrounding the second book.

Also, thank you to my editors, Miss Lyons and Wendy Porter, this book would not make sense if it were not for the many hours you put in editing. Your guidance and knowledge of the world of Grammar is very much appreciated. Thank you for your time and your support.

Thank you to those of you who have contacted me with your kind words about *Illusion*. Your thoughts, comments, and ideas always make me smile. I am glad to know that *Illusion* had the same impact on you as it did on me. I hope *Echo* will inspire you even further to follow your dreams.

Thank you to my amazing family and friends who have been so encouraging. Without you all behind me, none of this would have been possible. Thank you, Mom and Dad, for teaching me to follow my dreams. Thanks to Mom for being the best "Momager" ever and helping me to get *Illusion* off the ground. Thank you, Matt, for believing in this book and encouraging me to share my story. Thank you, Dad, for always telling me how proud you are of this book and of me- it means the world to me. Thank you also to my Aunt Debi for believing in these books and for always being there for me.

And as always, thank you, God, for this wonderful gift you have given me. I don't know what I would do without being able to express myself through words like this. Thank you for the amazing opportunities you have given me through my writing. I owe all of this to you.

About the Author:

Nadette Rae Rodgers lives and writes in Pittsburgh, Pennsylvania. Her passion for writing developed at a very young age. She published her first novel, *Illusion*, at age eighteen. Her interest in dream analysis was the basis for this book series. Nadette's goal in publishing this series is that her journey as an author will inspire others to follow their dreams too.

Echo is the second book of the Illusion Trilogy and Nadette's second published work.

Find her at her blog: **www.nadetteraerodgers.wordpress.com**
Visit the Official Website of the Illusion Trilogy:
www.illusiontrilogy.weebly.com

Illusion (Book One) is available online at Amazon, Barnes & Noble, and CreateSpace in both paperback and Kindle editions.

Author's Note

To My Lovely Readers,

Thank you for reading this book! I hope that you enjoyed it, and liked reading deeper into Addison's story. I really enjoyed writing this instalment of the trilogy and cannot wait to begin writing the next book for you all.

If you liked the book, please leave a review on Amazon, Barnes & Noble, or Goodreads. Reviews help other readers choose which books to purchase and read, and they help the authors know what readers liked or did not like about their stories.

I got so many wonderful comments and emails from readers after *Illusion* came out! I took a lot of readers' suggestions and compliments into consideration as I wrote this book. I really wanted my readers to feel like they were a part of this whole journey with me.

So, now that you've finished *Echo,* I would absolutely love to hear from you!

Email me your thoughts here: nadetteraerodgers@gmail.com

Leave reviews for other readers to see here:

Illusion -https://www.amazon.com/dp/1532807511

Echo – https://www.amazon.com/dp/0692909788

Again, thank you all so much for your involvement in this journey! Always remember to follow your dreams! You can all do such great things in this life.

Happy Reading!

-- Nadette Rae

Echo Playlist

I always love to hear where author's get their inspiration when they write.

I am inspired by nature, the people in my life, and music.

Because the songs I listened to as I wrote this novel had such an impact on the emotions and backstories that come through in *Echo*, I wanted to share the songs with you all in hopes that their lyrics and melodies might inspire you too.

Much Love,
Nadette Rae

* * *

Sleepsong - Bastille

From the Ground Up - Dan + Shay

Déjà vu (The Voice Performance) -- Lauren Duski

Patience - Abandoning Sunday

The A Team -- Ed Sheeran

Amnesia -- 5 Seconds of Summer

Angel With a Shotgun —The Cab

Back to December - Taylor Swift

Both of Us —B.o.B ft. Taylor Swift

Close Your Eyes —Dan +Shay

Demons - Imagine Dragons (cover by Sam Tsui & Max Schneider)

Do I Wanna Know? - Arctic Monkeys

The Draw - Bastille

Give Me Love - Ed Sheeran

Somewhere Only We Know - Keane

Wide Awake - Katy Perry

Without You—Glee Cast

You Found Me - The Fray

Bird Set Free - Sia

A Drop In The Ocean - Ron Pope

Glowing in the Dark - The Girl and The Dreamcatcher

Skinny Love - Birdy

1901—Birdy
Fire and Rain – Birdy
Dark Paradise – Lana Del Rey
Heathens – Twenty One Pilots
That Ghost – Megan & Liz
Little Do You Know – Alex & Sierra
Take Me to Church – Hozier
Jackie and Wilson – Hozier
Kiss Me Slowly – Parachute
Unsteady – X Ambassadors
I Heard Goodbye – Dan +Shay
Haunt – Bastille
Oblivion – Bastille
Teenage Dream – Katy Perry
Unwell – Matchbox Twenty
Tired- Alan Walker ft. Gavin James

Made in the USA
Columbia, SC
14 July 2017